Praise for

When Zachary Beaver Came to Town

Winner of the National Book Award
for Young People's Literature

An ALA Notable Book

One of ALA's Top Ten Best Books for Young Adults

A *Horn Book* Fanfare Selection

A *School Library Journal* Best Book of the Year

An *American Bookseller* "Pick of the Lists"

♦ "A master at finding the extraordinary in the ordinary . . . Holt reinvents the coming-of-age story, breathing life into a quirky cast of characters."

—*Kirkus Reviews*, pointer

★ "In her own down-to-earth, people-smart way, Holt offers a gift. . . . It is a lovely—at times even giddy—date with real life." —*The Horn Book*, starred review

★ "Holt humanizes the outsider without sentimentality. . . . In the tradition of many Southern writers, Holt reveals the freak in all of us, and the power of redemption."

—*Booklist*, starred review

★ "Holt has crafted a remarkable story about finding yourself by opening up to the people around you. An excellent choice to read alone or aloud."

—*School Library Journal*, starred review

★ "[Holt's] heartwarming and carefully crafted novel . . . drives home the point that everyday life is studded with memorable moments."

—*Publishers Weekly*, starred review

KIMBERLY WILLIS HOLT

WHEN ZACHARY BEAVER CAME TO TOWN

SQUARE FISH

HENRY HOLT AND COMPANY

NEW YORK

SQUARE
FISH
An Imprint of Macmillan
175 Fifth Avenue
New York, NY 10010
mackids.com

WHEN ZACHARY BEAVER CAME TO TOWN.

Printed in the United States of America by
R. R. Donnelley & Sons Company, Harrisonburg, Virginia.

Library of Congress Cataloging-in-Publication Data
Holt, Kimberly Willis.
When Zachary Beaver came to town / Kimberly Willis Holt.
p. cm.
Summary: During the summer of 1971 in a small Texas town, thirteen-year-old Toby and his best friend, Cal, meet the star of a sideshow act, 600-pound Zachary, the fattest boy in the world.
ISBN 978-1-250-06155-3 (15th Anniv. Ed.)
[1. Best friends—Fiction. 2. Friendship—Fiction. 3. Overweight persons—Fiction.
4. City and town life—Texas—Fiction. 5. Texas—Fiction.] I. Title.
PZ7.H74023Wh 1999 [Fic]—dc21 99-27998

Originally published in the United States by
Christy Ottaviano Books/Henry Holt and Company
First Square Fish Edition: 2011
Square Fish 15th Anniversary Edition: 2014
Square Fish logo designed by Filomena Tuosto

1 3 5 7 9 10 8 6 4 2

AR: 4.5 / F&P: Y / LEXILE: 700L

For

Christy Ottaviano

and

Jennifer Flannery

Chapter One

Nothing ever happens in Antler, Texas. Nothing much at all. Until this afternoon, when an old blue Thunderbird pulls a trailer decorated with Christmas lights into the Dairy Maid parking lot. The red words painted on the trailer cause quite a buzz around town, and before an hour is up, half of Antler is standing in line with two dollars clutched in hand to see the fattest boy in the world.

Since it's too late in the summer for firecrackers and too early for the Ladybug Waltz, Cal and I join Miss Myrtie Mae and the First Baptist Quilting Bee at the back of the line.

Miss Myrtie Mae wears a wide-brimmed straw hat. She claims that she's never exposed her skin to sun. Even so, wrinkles fold into her face like an unironed shirt. She takes her job as town historian and librarian seriously, and as usual, her camera hangs around her neck. "Toby, how's your mom?"

"Fine," I say.

"That will really be something if she wins."

"Yes, ma'am, it will." My mouth says the words, but my mind is not wanting to settle on a picture of her winning. Mom dreams of following in the footsteps of her favorite singer, Tammy Wynette. Last month she entered a singing contest in Amarillo and won first place. She got a trophy and an all-expense-paid trip to Nashville for a week to enter the National Amateurs' Country Music Competition at the Grand Ole Opry. The winner gets to cut a record album.

Cars and pickups pull into the Dairy Maid parking lot. Some people make no bones about it. They just get in line to see him. Others try to act like they don't know anything about the buzz. They enter the Dairy Maid, place their orders, and exit with Coke floats, chocolate-dipped cones, or curlicue fries, then wander to the back of the line. They don't fool me.

The line isn't moving because the big event hasn't started. Some skinny guy wearing a tuxedo, smoking a pipe, is taking the money and giving out green tickets. Cal could stand in line forever to relieve his curiosity. He knows more gossip than any old biddy in Antler because he gathers it down at the cotton gin, where his dad and the other farmers drink coffee.

"I got better things to do than this," I tell Cal. Like eat. My stomach's been growling all the time now because I haven't had a decent meal since Mom left a few days ago. Not that she cooked much lately since she was getting ready for that stupid contest. But I miss the fried catfish and barbecue dinners she brought home from the Bowl-a-Rama Cafe, where she works.

"Oh, come on, Toby," Cal begs. "He'll probably move out tomorrow and we'll never get another chance."

"He's just some fat kid. Heck, Malcolm Clifton probably has him beat hands down." Malcolm's mom claims he's big boned, not fat, but we've seen him pack away six jumbo burgers. I sigh real big like my dad does when he looks at my report card filled with Cs. "Okay," I say. "But I'm only waiting ten more minutes. After that, I'm splitting."

Cal grins that stupid grin with his black tooth showing. He likes to brag that he got his black tooth playing football, but I know the real story. His sister, Kate, socked him good when he scratched up her Carole King album. Cal says he was sick of hearing "You Make Me Feel Like a Natural Woman" every stinking day of his life.

Scarlett Stalling walks toward the line, holding her bratty sister Tara's hand. Scarlett looks cool wearing a bikini top underneath an open white blouse and hip huggers that hit right below her belly button. With her golden tan and long, silky blond hair, she could do a commercial for Coppertone.

Scarlett doesn't go to the back of the line. She walks over to me. *To me.* Smiling, flashing that Ultra Brite sex appeal smile and the tiny gap between her two front teeth. Cal grins, giving her the tooth, but I lower my eyelids half-mast and jerk my head back a little as if to say, "Hey."

Then she speaks. "Hey, Toby, would ya'll do me a favor?"

"Sure," I squeak, killing my cool act in one split second.

Scarlett flutters her eyelashes, and I suck in my breath. "Take Tara in for me." She passes her little sister's sticky hand like she's handing over a dog's leash. Then she squeezes her fingers into her pocket and pulls out two crumpled dollar bills. I would give anything to be one of those lucky dollar bills tucked into her pocket.

She flips back her blond mane. "I've got to get back home and get ready. Juan's dropping by soon."

The skin on my chest prickles. Mom is right. Scarlett Stalling is a flirt. Mom always told me, "You better stay a spittin' distance from that girl. Her mother had a bad reputation when I went to school, and the apple doesn't fall far from the tree."

Cal punches my shoulder. "Great going, ladies' man!"

I watch Scarlett's tight jeans sway toward her house so she can get ready for the only Mexican guy in Antler Junior High. Juan already shaves. He's a head taller than the rest of the guys (two heads taller than me). That gives him an instant ticket to play first string on our basketball team, even though he's slow footed and a lousy shot. Whenever I see him around town, a number-five-iron golf club swings at his side. I don't plan to ever give him a reason to use it.

"Fatty, fatty, two by four," Tara chimes as she stares at the trailer. "Can't get through the kitchen door."

"Shut up, squirt," I mutter.

Miss Myrtie Mae frowns at me.

Tara yanks on my arm. "Uummmm!" she hollers. "You said shut up. Scarlett!" She rises on her toes as if that makes her louder. "Toby said shut up to me!"

But it's too late. Scarlett has already disappeared across the street. She's probably home smearing gloss on those pouty lips while I hold her whiny sister's lollipop fingers, standing next to my black-toothed best friend, waiting to see the fattest boy in the world.

Chapter Two

There's not a cloud in the sky, and it's boiling hot. Wylie Womack's snow cone stand is across the parking lot, under the giant elm tree, and the idea is real tempting to let go of Tara's hand and bolt for it. But that would kill any chance I would ever have with Scarlett.

Sheriff Levi Fetterman drives by, making his afternoon rounds. He slows down and looks our way. His riding dog, Duke, sits in the passenger seat. Duke is Sheriff Levi's favorite adoptee. Anytime someone in Antler finds a stray cat or dog, they call the sheriff to pick up the animal and take it to the pound. Sheriff Levi can't bear to dump a dog, and because of that he has a couple dozen living on his one-acre place a mile out of town. However, cats are a different story. They go straight to the pound.

Sheriff Levi waves at us, then heads on his way. He drives all the way down Main Street and turns toward the highway.

Finally the skinny guy selling tickets moves to the top step in front of the trailer door. Even though he smokes a pipe, his baby face, braces, and tux make him look like he's ready for the eighth-grade formal. From the front his hair looks short, but he turns and I notice a ponytail hangs down his back.

"Welcome, fine folks," he yells like a carnival barker. His voice is older than his face—deep and clear like a DJ's. "Step this way to see Zachary Beaver, the fattest boy in the world. Six hundred and forty-three pounds. You don't have to rush, but keep in mind others behind you want a look too. My name is Paulie Rankin, and I'll be happy to take your questions."

"And your money too," Cal says out of the corner of his mouth. "By the way, can you loan me two bucks?" I nod and peel two dollars from my wallet.

Tara jumps and jumps. "I can't wait! I can't wait! Do you think he's fatter than Santa?"

"How would I know?" I grumble.

Cal kneels next to her. "I'll bet he's three times fatter than Santa."

Her eyes grow big. "Oooh! That's *real* fat."

Cal likes little kids, but then, he sometimes acts

like one. Maybe because he's the youngest in the family. He has two brothers and one sister. His oldest brother, Wayne, is in the army, serving in Vietnam. He's the kind of big brother I wish I had.

Wayne writes to Cal every week. But Cal is so lazy, he hardly ever writes him back. If I had a brother in Vietnam that wrote me letters saying what a neat brother I was, I'd always write him back.

Cal reads every letter to me. Wayne never says anything about the kind of stuff we see on the news—no blood and guts. He writes about home. How he misses lying in bed, listening to Casey Kasem and Wolfman Jack on the radio. How he wishes he could eat a Bahama Mama snow cone from Wylie Womack's stand and let the syrup run down his fingers. And how the worst day of his life, before he got drafted, was the day he missed catching that fly ball during the Bucks-Cardinals game because he was too busy watching some girl walk up the stands in her pink hot pants. He says he'd live that day over a hundred times if it meant he could come back home. Wayne makes Antler sound like the best place on the face of the earth. Sometimes he even adds: *P.S. Tell your buddy Toby I said hey.*

The line moves slowly, and when people exit the trailer, some come out all quiet like they've been shaken up at a revival. A few say things like, "Lord-a-mercy!" Others joke and laugh.

Finally we make it to the front door. I hand Paulie Rankin four bucks and glance down at Tara. Legs crossed, she's bouncing like crazy.

Paulie pulls the pipe out of his mouth. "Hey, the kid doesn't have to *go*, does she?"

"Do you?" I ask her, not intending to sound as mean as it comes out.

She shakes her head, making her two tiny blond ponytails flop like puppy ears.

"She better not," says Paulie. He rubs his chin and watches her suspiciously as we climb the trailer steps.

I grit my teeth and repeat Paulie's warning. "You better not."

The cramped trailer smells like Pine-Sol and lemon Pledge and it's dark except for a lamp and sunlight slipping between the crack in the curtains. A drape hangs at one end, hiding the space behind it. And in the middle of the trailer sits the largest human being I've ever seen. Zachary Beaver is the size of a two-man pup tent. His short black hair tops his huge moon face like a snug cap that's two sizes too small. His skin is pale as buttermilk, and his hazel eyes are practically lost in his puffy cheeks.

Wearing huge pull-on pants and a brown T-shirt, he sits in front of a television, watching *Password*, drinking a giant chocolate milk shake. A *TV Guide* rests on his lap, and a few stacks of books and *Newsweek* magazines are at his feet along with a sack of Lay's potato chips. Three Plexiglas walls box him in. The walls aren't very high, but I figure they keep brats like Tara from poking him. After all, he's not the Pillsbury Doughboy. A sign in the corner of one wall reads, Don't Touch the Glass, but if someone does, a squirt bottle of glass cleaner and a roll of paper towels are next to the TV.

There's no denying it—this place is clean with a capital *C*. And with the exception of a dusty bookcase filled with encyclopedias and other books, it's as sterile as a hospital. A gold cardboard box is on the center shelf by itself.

It seems weird, standing here, staring at someone because they look different. Wylie Womack is the strangest-looking person in Antler, but I'm so used to seeing his crooked body riding around town in his beat-up golf cart that I don't think about him looking weird.

Miss Myrtie Mae steps forward, lifting her camera. "Mind if I take a few pictures?"

"Yes, I do," the fat kid says.

Miss Myrtie Mae lets the camera drop to her chest. "You like books, I see. I work at the Antler library."

Zachary Beaver ignores her.

For once Tara is quiet, but Cal is anything but speechless. He wants to know everything. Like a redheaded woodpecker, he *pecks, pecks, pecks,* trying to make a dent.

"How much do you eat?" he asks Zachary.

"As much as I can."

"How old are you?"

"Old enough."

"Where do you go to school?"

"You're looking at it." Zachary never once smiles or looks us in the eye. He focuses on that game show.

Then Cal asks, "What's in the gold box?"

Zachary ignores him, his gaze dragging across Cal's face.

I wish Cal would shut up. Besides embarrassing me, his questions sound mean. But Zachary only looks bored and kind of irritated, like someone swishing away a fly.

I don't ask questions, but I think them. Like how did he get inside the trailer? He's way too wide to fit through the door. Tara's stupid chant plays over and over in my mind. *Fatty, fatty, two by four. Can't get through the kitchen door.* I'm surprised she hasn't started singing it. I look down at her. Her bugged-out eyes water, and one hand covers her mouth. The other is locked between her crossed legs. A yellow stream trickles down her leg and wets her white Keds.

I jump back. "Jeez—!"

Zachary looks up from the TV, his eyes flashing, his wide nostrils flaring. "Do I smell pee? Did that kid pee in here?" He points toward the exit, the flesh on his arm flapping as he punches his finger in the air. "Get her outta here!"

Every eye in the trailer stares at us. Except Cal, who is snooping around, picking up stuff. I want to yank Tara by her ponytails, punt her like a football, and send her sailing through the air, across the street, toward her house to knock down Juan as he arrives at Scarlett's door. Instead I grab Tara by the hand—the one that covers her mouth—and whip through the exit, past the waiting crowd. Taking long strides so that Tara must run to keep from falling, I cross two streets to her house, where Juan sits on the left side of the porch swing, holding Scarlett's hand. His number-five iron is at his feet, and he wears a white T-shirt with *Don't Mess with Super Mex* printed in ink across the front.

"He was soooo fat!" yells Tara, running inside their

house. A great big wet spot covers the rear end of her shorts.

This has got to be my lowest moment ever. I swerve around, trying to avoid Juan and Scarlett.

But it's too late. Juan calls out, "Hey, man, I didn't know you baby-sat."

Chapter Three

Seeing Scarlett and Juan together rattles me so bad, I almost forget my bike parked in front of the Dairy Maid. By the time I get back, the line has died down and Cal is gone. I hop on my bike, ride past the town square, and head home.

Antler is off Highway 287, tucked between the railroad tracks and the breaks of Palo Duro Canyon. Because of the breaks, it's not as flat and sparse as most of the Panhandle. Most Panhandle towns don't have trees unless someone planted them, but Antler has plenty of elms and cedars.

Our town's population has been shrinking since the bank foreclosed on some of the farms. A lot of the stores are vacant. Ferris Kelly's Bowl-a-Rama, Earline's Real Estate Agency, and Clifton's Dry Goods remain. Antique shops started opening in some of the vacant stores a couple of years ago.

The majority of the people who shop at the antique stores are passing through from Fort Worth or Dallas. Which is weird because they look like they can afford new stuff.

A cotton gin sits at the outskirts of Antler, and it isn't unusual to see a speck of cotton surfing on the wind like a lost snowflake.

Our house on Ivy Street is four streets away from the square and two streets from the school. Even though Cal's family owns a cotton farm on the edge of town, they live next door to us in a small brick house. It doesn't seem fair—Cal's family stuffed in their little place like sardines while the three of us live in a big two-story.

Not that our house is a mansion or anything. Mom calls it a hand-me-down. First it belonged to Mom's grandparents, then her parents, now us. It looks like the kind of place you'd see on a farm surrounded by acres of land—a white clapboard with a wraparound porch and a weather vane on the roof.

When I reach home, I see Cal's bike lying flat in his yard. His brother Billy is working on Wayne's old Mustang in their driveway. He's trying to get it fixed up to surprise Wayne when he comes home in March.

A flag waves from a tall pole in their front yard. Before Wayne went to Vietnam, they only hung it on the Fourth of July and other patriotic holidays. Now the flag goes up every morning and comes down each night.

Cal's mom, Mrs. McKnight, is pruning her roses in their front yard while she hums a song. I listen close, but I don't know the tune. Maybe it's an old Irish song. Cal says his mom's family passed them down like an old quilt.

As usual, Mrs. McKnight wears a floral apron tied around her waist. She's the only one in Cal's family who isn't redheaded. Right now her black hair blows wildly in the breeze. It makes me think how Mom puts so much hair spray on hers it defies any Panhandle wind and teases it so high it could hide a Frisbee. Mom claims big hair helps her hit the high notes.

Mrs. McKnight waves, and I wave back. "Any word from your mom?"

"Not yet." I wish everyone would stop asking me about Mom. She only left a few days ago, and the contest isn't until next Thursday. After Thursday they'll ask, "How did she do?" At least that fat guy replaced Mom as the juiciest news in town.

At home, Mozart plays from the stereo while Dad stands at the sink, slicing bell peppers. He's wearing his post office uniform with his black Bic pens neatly lined up in his shirt pocket. His head is bent, and I notice his bald spot has grown to the size of an orange. Radishes, onions, and lettuce from his backyard garden lie on the counter. Dad's fingers are long and straight. As postmaster he sorts mail at the post office as quick as a card shark deals out a deck. But right now, cutting those peppers, his fingers look clumsy and awkward. "Hungry?" he asks.

"Yeah, I guess."

"I thought I'd make a salad." Dad may grow the vegetables, but he's never made a salad in his life. He looks lost in the kitchen, digging around for a salad bowl. He opens a cabinet, scratches his chin, then selects another door. I don't know where to find a bowl either. I search in the pantry. The shelves are filled with food. Boxes of cereal, pasta, and crackers, cans of soup, stewed tomatoes, and green peas. I open the refrigerator. Milk, eggs, and American cheese slices are jammed next to packages of ham and bologna. Dad always griped at the way Mom never kept enough groceries in the house. Now she's prepared us for a national disaster.

All that food reminds me of the night she packed for her trip. I sat on the edge of her bed, watching her. Every pair of cowboy boots she owned lined the wall, including the turquoise ones with red stars. She flung all her western shirts and skirts on the bed and dropped lipstick tubes from under her sink into a small suitcase. I swear she packed like she was going for the whole summer instead of a week. About the only thing she didn't pack was the pearl necklace that once belonged to her mom. She told me that someday she'd give it to the woman I married so it would stay in the family. Mom sang "Hey, Good Lookin' " as she packed, and the entire time I couldn't help wondering if moms were supposed to be that happy to get away. Mrs. McKnight doesn't go on trips without her family.

Dad has already set the table with Mom's vinyl Las Vegas show scene place mats. Elvis in a white glittered suit looks up at me, microphone in hand. The table seems enormous without Mom sitting at her place. And it's quiet. Mom did all the talking at dinner. While Dad and I ate, she'd tell us something funny the Judge, Miss Myrtie Mae's senile brother, said that day at the cafe. Or how Sheriff Levi finally ordered something different from the menu, only to quickly change it back to his usual—hamburger with jalapeños and French fries.

I always knew Mom dreamed of being a famous singer, but I guess I thought it was only a dream. The kind of thing you wish for upon a star, but deep down you know it probably won't ever come true. After all, stars are a long ways away.

Dad's salad really isn't bad if you take out the onions. They smell strong, but I eat around them. He looks like he's waiting for me to mention the salad, so I tell him, "Pretty good, Dad."

"Really?" He sounds relieved, and I'm glad I said something.

"Yeah."

"I didn't use too many onions?"

I look down at the sliced onions around the edge of my plate. "Well, I've never been crazy about onions anyway."

"I'll try and remember next time."

I want to say, Don't sweat it, Dad. Mom will be back soon enough. No need turning into a gourmet chef.

Dad might as well be from Pluto as from Dallas. People in Antler see it as the same thing. The funny thing is, now it seems like Dad belongs here more than Mom. I don't think she ever counted on him settling in Antler when he passed through years ago, looking for a place to raise worms.

Dad is the Otto Wilson part of Otto Wilson's Tennessee Brown Nose Fishing Worms. He keeps most of the bait shops stocked from here to Lake Kiezer and Lake Seymour. He also raises enough for the local men heading out to their favorite fishing holes. I help take care of the worms—separating them by size, changing their soil and keeping it moist.

After dinner Dad and I do the dishes while we listen to the television news. We stand side by side; I barely reach his shoulder. People say I take after Mom—blond, brown eyed, and *small.*

When the war correspondent comes on, the volume gets louder. The reporter hollers into his microphone, trying to be heard over the sounds of helicopters and M-16s in the background.

Dad turns around and glances at the television screen. "Turn that crap off, will you?"

As I walk toward the TV, I wonder if Wayne is there or someplace like it.

Later I ride my bike past the town limits to Gossimer Lake. Dusk has arrived, and even though the sun is sinking below the horizon, I can see the moon. I pass the Dairy Maid, where the crowd has left. Now that it's dark, the Christmas lights glow like fallen stars strung around the trailer. Paulie Rankin sits outside his Thunderbird in a lawn chair, smoking his pipe and gazing up at the sky. I guess he'll head out in the morning to the next town full of suckers with two dollars to burn.

What a sorry life Zachary Beaver must have, sitting every day in a cramped trailer while people come by to gawk at him. But at least he goes places. At least he doesn't watch the girl of his dreams hold hands with some other guy or have a mom who's off becoming Tammy Wynette. Except for having Cal, life in Antler is about as exciting as watching worms mate. And Cal can be such a dork. He may be the reason I'm batting a big fat zero with Scarlett. Maybe he's ruining my image.

Gossimer Lake is more like a large pond. It started out as a puny mud puddle. One spring we had an unusual amount of rain, and a mud puddle on Henrick Gossimer's land grew to the size of a kiddie pool. Mr. Gossimer said he thought it was the Lord's way of saying he should do something for Antler's young folks. He dug the ground around the puddle as much as he could, then he called on Mr. Owens to bulldoze the rest.

Pretty soon it became a town project. The First Baptist men's group built a small dam to keep in the water, and the Shriners club raised a windmill to keep the lake filled. That's how dried-up Antler got its man-made lake. It's about as good as a mud puddle, though. Signs posted everywhere read, No Swimming. No Fishing. They might as well post one that reads, No Fun Allowed.

I dodge the trees that fringe the lake, jump off my

bike, and flop on the grass near the edge of the water. A light breeze blows from the southwest, bringing the stink of the Martins' cattle feedlot. I take off my sneakers and socks and roll up my jeans. Once Cal and I waded into the water, but when Cal said, "I wonder if there's any snakes in here?" I jumped out and he quickly followed. Tonight I don't care if a snake pit is at the bottom of this giant puddle. Let them bite.

Just as I step into the water, I hear grass rustle and I decide maybe I'm not sold on seeing a snake after all. Across the lake, two figures sit close to each other. One of them moves, and I see a glimmer of blond hair. My stomach feels sick as my eyes zero in on Scarlett and Juan.

Chapter Four

The next morning I jolt from a deep sleep. Dirt clods thump against my bedroom window, and Cal is calling my name. When I pull up my shade, light spills into the room. I have to squint real hard to see Cal looking up at me from the ground.

"Come on!" he hollers. "You going to sleep all day?"

It's only eight in the morning. With Cal McKnight as my best friend, I don't need an alarm clock. His family has a morning routine. Everyone up by 6 A.M., no matter if it's summer—beds made, breakfast eaten, dishes washed and put away, teeth brushed by six-thirty, then on to the chore list attached to the refrigerator with a smiley face magnet. The list has three columns, with each McKnight kid's name (except Wayne's) at the top—Kate, Billy, and Cal. Whenever I spend the night with Cal, I get thrown into their routine. But I don't mind. They seem like a happy army on a mission, zipping through their list.

In the summer they're out the door by eight, with hoes in their hands, headed to work in their cotton field. Most of the cotton farmers use herbicide to control weeds and insecticide to get rid of the bugs. Except for releasing the ladybugs in his fields once a year, Mr. McKnight doesn't use anything. He believes a penny saved is a penny earned.

Once Mom looked out the kitchen window and shook her head when she saw Cal, Kate, and Cal's brothers piling into the back of the pickup with their tools. "Charlie McKnight works his kids like slaves. He has hired help to do that." Mom believes a penny earned is a penny spent at Clifton's Dry Goods.

But today is Saturday, and even Cal's dad gives his kids the weekend off. I yawn, stretch, and tell Cal to wait. Then I straighten the green plastic soldiers lined up on my dresser and cross yesterday off the calendar. Two hundred thirty-one more days until Wayne comes home. After stumbling into a T-shirt and jeans, I grab two English muffins and go outside. I need to wet down the worms' dirt, but Dad won't mind if I do it later as long as it's done today.

Cal waits on his bike, hands gripping the handlebars

so tight, his knuckles turn white. "Hey, snoozer, what took you so long?"

I ignore him, toss him a muffin, and head to the garage to get my own bike. Next door, Kate tries to parallel park the McKnight station wagon between two garbage cans set on the street. She looks like an old lady—frizzy red hair twisted in a knot on top of her head, glasses low on her nose, shoulders hiked up to her ears, and her body curled over the steering wheel.

Every high school junior in Antler already has their driver's license except for Kate. Mrs. McKnight drove her to Amarillo three times this summer to take the test, and each time Kate failed the driving part because she can't parallel park. Now she frantically looks from the rearview mirror to the side mirror, inching the car backward.

Watching from my driveway, Cal and I straddle our bikes and eat our dry muffins. I stop chewing. I even cross my fingers, wanting for her to succeed this time. But as usual, she backs into the rear garbage can, knocking it over, causing the metal to clank against the road.

"Oh!" Cal smacks his hands against his chest and falls off his bike in slow motion. "She got me, buddy."

Flat on his back, the rear tire covering his legs, he raises his head and looks her way. I laugh.

Kate jumps out of the station wagon, pushes up her glasses, and returns the can to its upright position. Her baggy jeans and tie-dyed T-shirt swallow her skinny body. Before getting back behind the wheel, she faces Cal, tight fists at her sides, and glares.

"Come on," Cal says. "Let's get out of here before she blows."

We race down the sidewalks on Ivy Street, Cal on the right side of the road, me on the left. We jump curbs like track stars leaping hurdles. We take sharp turns at the corner of Ivy and Langston, leaning into the wind, knowing we won't fall because we've done it a million times before. We can stop our bikes on a dime, and we do when we reach the school. In a few months the grounds will be crawling with kids, but right now Malcolm is mowing it with his dad's riding mower. From the looks of it, he's been at it awhile, and the smell of freshly cut grass floats in the air. He waves and we wave back, but Cal yells, "Hey, Malcolm. You big goofball! Crybaby!"

We're safe because Malcolm can't hear Cal through the motor's growl. He waves again, sucks in his big gut, and accelerates like he's on a Harley-Davidson.

He's wearing his Antler Wrestling T-shirt, but the only wrestling action Malcolm has seen is from the bench.

Last summer the three of us were out by Sheriff Levi's place with the electric fence surrounding it. Cal and I challenged Malcolm to a pissing contest. We stood facing the fence, only Cal and I undershot. As we predicted, show-off Malcolm aimed for the fence, and as soon as he successfully hit his target, he was knocked flat on his back. It didn't really hurt him, but the shock shook him up bad. He had hollered, "A snake! I got bit by a snake!" Cal and I split a gut laughing, but Malcolm ran home crying to his mother. We were grounded for weeks.

"How much do you think that guy eats?" Cal asks.

"Malcolm?" I ask.

"No," Cal says, shaking his head. "Zachary Beaver."

"He told you. As much as he can."

"Man, that guy was huge," Cal continues. "I wonder if he's in the *Guinness Book of World Records.*"

"Who cares?"

"Do you think he really weighs 643 pounds?"

I shrug. "I don't know. I guess."

"I mean, how do they weigh him? Most scales don't go that high."

"Maybe they weigh him at a meat market."

Cal scratches his chin. "I wonder how he goes to the bathroom?"

"How do *you* go to the bathroom?"

"You know what I mean. I mean, does he have to have a special toilet?"

I roll my eyes.

"And what do you think he keeps in that gold cardboard box?"

I don't want to talk about the fat kid. It makes my stomach ache because it reminds me of what happened with Tara, and that reminds me of seeing Scarlett and Juan at the lake last night.

"Where to now?" I ask.

"How about Wylie's?"

"It's too early for a snow cone," I say. "Besides, he doesn't open until one."

"Swimming?"

I throw him a steely gaze. He knows better. I haven't been swimming at the town pool since last summer, when I swallowed a bunch of pool water and started choking. The lifeguard got excited and yanked me out of the pool and did mouth-to-mouth resuscitation.

"Oh, yeah," Cal remembers. "Bowling?"

"I guess." Nothing sounds particularly fun this morning. The wind has started to kick up, and Cal's red curls blow around his face.

"Did your mom win?"

"For the hundredth time, the contest isn't until next Thursday night."

"You got cash?" Cal asks, not a bit embarrassed.

"Some. Not enough for both of us."

"Then I better stop home first. Sure hope Kate has cooled off."

"You're going to hit her up for money?"

"Have to. Billy is as broke as me. He sinks every penny he makes at the drive-in into Wayne's old junker. Kate saves money like Scrooge."

"Man, you're brave."

Cal never has money with him. He usually bums some off me, then forgets to pay me back. One day when I was mad at him, I added up every single cent I loaned him since fifth grade. Forty-six bucks. We made up the next day, so I never told him.

When we return, the McKnights' station wagon is parked in the driveway and the garbage cans are gone. Inside their house, the *Sound of Music* album plays in the background. Next to Carole King, Kate likes show tunes best.

Kate hunches over her sewing machine at the

dining-room table. Billy sleeps on the couch, oblivious to the music and the growl of the machine.

Cal walks over to Kate and grabs a piece of blue shiny fabric pinned to a pattern section on the table.

"Put that down!" she snaps.

Holding the piece to his chest, he skips around the room like a sissy, singing with the music, "I am sixteen going on seventeen." It would have been funny except Kate didn't deserve it. I want to tell her—I'm not like him. I think he's acting like a jerk too.

Kate jumps to her feet, but her shoulders remain hunched. Her face tense, she pushes at the POW bracelets she wears on each arm. Most girls have only one. Not Kate. She says, if some guys are being held prisoner in Vietnam, the least she can do is wear their names on her wrists. "Put it down, Cal Michael McKnight, right this instant! Or else!"

Billy doesn't stir. He even starts to snore. I stand there, helpless. I dread these moments when Cal torments Kate for no reason. She really isn't all that bad.

Kate chases Cal and yanks the fabric out of his hand. The pattern rips and the fabric drops to the floor. Kate's eyes bulge. "Now look what you've done."

"Whoops," Cal says. "I guess this means you won't loan me three bucks."

She grabs the fabric off the ground. "Get out of this

house, Cal McKnight, or I'll throw you out on your skinny butt!"

Billy's eyes pop wide, and without bothering to find out why Kate's freaking out, he yells, "Get out, Cal. You punk!"

Cal pulls my shirt as he bolts from the room and heads for the front door. We hop on our bikes and pedal like crazy, the wind smacking our faces. We ride along in silence with only the sound of our tires meeting the pavement. From a distance, I hear the train pulling into the depot. "When are the ladybugs getting here?"

"Dad said probably next week sometime."

Last year the ladybugs arrived closer to the Fourth of July. Now I wonder if it will be too late for the ladybugs to get rid of the bollworms. I guess I'm excited because this will be the first year that Cal and I get to empty the sacks of ladybugs in the field. "Where to now?" I ask.

"Let's go to the Bowl-a-Rama." That's what's boring about living in Antler. There's only a handful of things to do, and when we don't have money for those things, we usually go anyway and watch other people do them.

The Bowl-a-Rama sits across the street from the Dairy Maid. As we approach, I'm surprised to see the trailer still parked in the lot. But this time something is missing—Paulie Rankin's blue Thunderbird.

Cal and I stop pedaling at the same time and stare at the trailer. "Maybe they went to another town to eat," I say.

"Do you think *he's* still there?" Cal asks. "I mean, the fat kid?"

"Nah," I say, but I wonder too. "Come on. It's too hot to stay out here." We park our bikes on the sidewalk and head inside.

The Bowl-a-Rama smells of sweaty feet and cigarettes, but it's the coldest place in town. Today the air conditioner is cranked so high, goose bumps pop out on my arms. Two of the six lanes broke last summer, but Ferris hasn't bothered to have them fixed.

Ferris leans against the counter, where the bowling shoes are kept, rubbing his long Elvis sideburns. With his shirtsleeves rolled up, his two tattoos are visible. One is an anchor, the other a hula girl. He said he got them the night he met Jim Beam. Cal thought he was talking about a real person until I explained that Jim Beam was whiskey and Ferris was drunk as a skunk when he got the tattoos. That was before Ferris met Jesus and got religion.

Ferris is staring out the window, and it takes him a

moment to recognize us. Finally he rubs his eyes with his thumb and finger. "Hey, fellas, if you stare into the sun too long, it'll blind ya." He yawns and scratches his day-old whiskers, making a *wisk-wisk* sound. "How's your mom, Toby?"

"Great." I guess.

"Well, the next time she calls, you tell her that her job is waiting for her. After all, where else can folks in Antler get a meal with free entertainment?"

Mom is known as the singing waitress. She makes up songs for the customers, and if they're a pain, she makes up songs *about* them. Her voice is high and strong with just the right twang. She may sing songs about honky-tonk angels while serving Bowl-a-Rama specials, but in her mind she's probably on the stage of the Grand Ole Opry.

In the cafe, next to the picture of the Lord's Supper, Ferris hung a huge banner above the soda fountain counter—Good Luck, Opalina!

Ferris comes out from behind the counter, limping to the door and turning the Open sign around to face the front. The talk around town is his limp was a self-inflicted wound so he didn't have to serve in the Korean War. Ferris claims it was a pure coincidence that he was cleaning his gun the day before he was to report for active duty.

Before that happened, Ferris wanted to be a preacher. He even went a semester to a Bible college in Oklahoma. Now he never goes to church, but Mom says he knows the Bible from Genesis to Revelation. It's almost as hard for me to picture Ferris a preacher as it is believing he'd ever ditch a war.

Cal hops on the counter. "What's up, Ferris?"

"Oh, nothing much in here. But I've been curious about what's going on across the street."

"How's that?" I prop my elbow on the counter and rest my chin on my fist.

"That freak show fella took off in his Thunderbird about an hour ago."

"Did the fat guy go with him?" Cal asks, hopping off the counter.

"Don't think so," Ferris says. "That's what's got me to wonderin'. Thought they'd be pulling out by now."

Cal heads for the door. He glances back and waves his arm in giant sweeps. "Come on."

Underneath the trailer, a hose and wire stretch across the parking lot to the inside of the Dairy Maid. Paulie Rankin must have worked out something for the electricity and water.

"Help me up," Cal says. And a minute later, Cal

sits on top of my shoulders, peeking through the crack between the drapes in the back window.

I get a weird feeling that maybe we shouldn't be doing this. My heart pounds like a ticking bomb.

"Cal, they arrest people for looking in windows. The fat kid could be taking a bath or something."

"Jeez!"

"The sheriff could drive by. He could slap handcuffs on us and haul our butts to the county jail."

"Mary, and Joseph!" Cal calls out.

My heart leaps into my throat, but I risk it and trade places with Cal to take a look.

It's the back of Zachary Beaver. Through the grimy streaked window, I watch him eating frosted cornflakes from a mixing bowl huge enough to hold two boxes of cereal. An opened book is on the table next to the bowl.

"Man, he can put it away, can't he?" Cal says loud enough for Zachary to turn around and yank back the curtain. I wiggle, trying to free Cal's grasp around my ankles, but instead Cal's grip tightens and together we fall to the asphalt.

"What are you looking at, perverts?" Zachary yells. And even though the window is closed, his words pierce through the glass and pound our ears. He slides open the window. "If you Peeping Toms don't get out of here, I'll call the cops."

Cal and I race to our bikes, accidentally grabbing each other's, not bothering to switch until we're safe at home.

Chapter Five

The day after Zachary Beaver caught Cal and me peeking into his trailer, we head over to the library to find out if he really is the fattest boy in the world. When I was little, Mom would take me there each week for Miss Myrtie Mae's story time, but I haven't stepped inside the library in ages. Neither has Cal.

We look through the door window. Miss Myrtie Mae sits behind an oak desk, peering over her wire-framed glasses, studying some black-and-white photos. She does a double take when we enter. "Haven't seen you boys in here in a decade. Anything I can help you with?"

"No, ma'am," we answer together, heading toward the other side of the room.

Dust particles spin under the overhead lights, and the moldy smell of old books fills the air. Cal and I wander around, our eyes scanning the shelves.

Treasure Island, the Hardy Boys Mysteries, and *Old Yeller* remind me of nights when Mom read to me before bedtime.

"It wouldn't be over here," I whisper. "This is fiction."

"Did you say something?" Miss Myrtie Mae asks.

I shake my head. "Oh, no, ma'am. I was talking to Cal."

She nods and looks down at the pictures.

I glance across the room. Letters cut from construction paper spell *Nonfiction* above a bookcase. The shelves contain books about rattlesnakes, space, and gemstones. There are also books about the American Revolutionary War and biographies on a few presidents. But there isn't a copy of the *Guinness Book of World Records.*

"It's not here," Cal says.

"Are you looking for this?" Miss Myrtie Mae asks, holding up a blue hardback book.

Cal steps up to her desk, and I follow. Miss Myrtie Mae holds out the *Guinness Book of World Records.* "Thanks!" Cal hollers.

"You're welcome," she says, returning to her photos. I nudge closer and notice her pictures of Zachary Beaver's trailer and of people waiting in line to see him.

I look over Cal's shoulder as he thumbs through the book.

"Pages fifteen and sixteen," says Miss Myrtie Mae, not even glancing up.

Cal turns to page fifteen and finds the subtitle "Heaviest Man."

I stare at Miss Myrtie Mae, puzzled. *How did she know?*

Her gray eyebrows hike above her glasses. "You think you're the first person who came sniffing around about that boy? I've seen more people in this library the last couple of days than I've seen all year."

"Oh," I say, embarrassed to be lumped in with the same group of nosy people.

"He's not in there," she states.

We keep reading, looking at the pictures, searching for anything about Zachary.

Miss Myrtie Mae shrugs. "Suit yourself."

She's right. The book lists that the fattest man now living is reported to weigh 739 pounds. It also shows a picture of the heaviest man of all time wearing a pair of gigantic overalls. The book says that at the time his picture was taken, he weighed seven hundred pounds. He died when he was thirty-two years old and was buried in a piano case. I wonder if that's Zachary Beaver's destiny.

"He's a lot bigger than Zachary Beaver," Cal says.

"Give him time," I say.

Cal scratches his head. "But if Zachary weighs 643 pounds, he should be near that size. He must be lying."

Miss Myrtie Mae's eyes narrow to staples. "What difference should it make? If he wants to call himself the fattest boy in the world, what harm is it doing to you?"

Cal and I don't answer. We hand back the book, thank her, and leave, ending our once-in-a-decade visit to the Antler Public Library.

For the first time in a year Dad treats me to lunch at the Bowl-a-Rama Cafe. Dad would just as soon eat paper than Ferris's greasy food. He believes you are what you eat. But he's in a good mood because "Super Mex" Lee Trevino won the British Open this weekend. When Trevino came on the pro golf circuit a few years ago, he was considered the underdog—a poor Mexican American guy from El Paso. Dad always roots for the underdogs. It doesn't matter where they're from. He cheered for the Boston Red Sox long before they won the American League pennant, in 67.

Before we enter the Bowl-a-Rama, I glance across the street. The trailer is still parked in the Dairy Maid parking lot and Paulie Rankin's car is still missing.

"Hey, Toby!" I hear Cal's voice, but I don't see him. I look up, shading my eyes from the sun. Cal perched on the roof of the Bowl-a-Rama, our getaway spot.

"Thought you'd be working."

"Dad gave me the day off because Kate went to take her driving test and Billy had to go to work early."

"Come join us for lunch, Cal," Dad says. "I'm treating."

Never one to turn down a free meal, Cal climbs down the metal ladder hooked on the side of the building.

"Does Ferris know you're up there?" Dad asks.

"He doesn't care," Cal says. "We do it all the time."

Dad examines me, eyebrows raised. "Oh?"

Cal smacks my back.

"Ow!"

"Paulie's car is still gone."

"I know, Cal. I've got eyes too."

As soon as we step inside the cafe, I breathe in the spicy smells. Ferris's chalkboard hangs near the kitchen window behind the counter. *Today's Special: Honey Fried Chicken, Corn Fritters, and Mustard Greens.* Beneath the menu is the daily Bible verse. *"It is an honor for a man to cease from strife: but every fool will be meddling." Proverbs 20:3.* Mom says some people wear their religion on their sleeves. Ferris posts his on the chalkboard.

Southern gospel music plays from the jukebox, but the sound of bowling balls hitting pins in the next room can still be heard. From the kitchen window, Ima Jean stares at us through her steamed-up cat-eyed glasses. With the back of her hand, she wipes them in a circular motion.

Ferris does a double take when he sees Dad. "How ya doing, Otto? Haven't seen you in a long time."

Dad nods toward Ferris. "Doing fine. Yourself?"

Ferris strokes his beard stubble. "Couldn't be better. Sure do miss your woman, though."

Dad glances at the Good Luck, Opalina! sign hanging over the counter. His temples pulse, and he averts his eyes to the floor. The ice machine moans, dropping a load of ice. We walk to a corner table, and Ferris limps our way with a menu. His watermelon belly hangs over his belt, and a patch of hairy skin peeks through a gap between two buttons.

Soon the regular lunch crowd begins to pour inside the cafe—the Shriners in their tall hats and decorated vests, the farmers with their sons, and Earline, the only real estate lady in Antler. In fact, that's what it says on her Volkswagen—Earline Carter, the Real

Estate Lady. As if in a town our size, we wouldn't know who she was. If she mashed down her black beehive hairdo, she would probably only be four feet tall. Today, despite all the hairpins and spray, her beehive is leaning like the Tower of Pisa. "Hello, Otto. How's Opalina?"

"Fine."

"I guess this is her shot at the big time, isn't it? She's a brave woman, going all the way to Nashville. Alone at that. You're mighty brave to let her." She raises her eyebrows, waiting.

A hush falls over the cafe, but Dad doesn't say anything. The only sound comes from the jukebox, where another record drops in place. Elvis begins singing "The Old Rugged Cross." Earline squirms and brushes imaginary lint off her sleeve.

Miss Myrtie Mae comes in the cafe with the Judge. He's been retired for years, but everyone still greets him that way. Like Miss Myrtie Mae, he's long and skinny, but a good ten years older than her. His thick white hair is combed back with no part and his cheeks sink into his face, forming valleys below his high cheekbones.

Miss Myrtie Mae selects the table in front of us. "Sit here, Brother." As always she wears her straw hat and pointy shoes.

The Judge settles in the chair and starts tinkering with his gold pocket watch. Miss Myrtie Mae nods at Dad. "Otto," she says, "Brother and I would sure appreciate it if Toby would mow our yard the rest of the summer. We'd pay him a fair price."

I wonder why she doesn't ask me, when I'm sitting right here.

Dad looks at me, eyebrows raised. "Toby?"

"Yes, ma'am. I'll be happy to mow it." There are worse things to do than mowing Miss Myrtie Mae's lawn—like taking care of worms. Besides, I could use the money.

Cal's face turns red as his hair. He's tapping a straw against his glass, and his tongue makes a lump in his cheek. It dawns on me that Billy mowed Miss Myrtie Mae's yard the last two summers and Wayne did it before that. I guess Cal thought he'd be the natural choice.

"Fridays be okay?" she asks.

"Yes, ma'am."

"Order out!" hollers Ima Jean through the window. Ferris heads over to pick up the plates.

Outside, I see Wylie Womack park his golf cart across the square in the shade of the giant elm, the same place he's parked every summer day I can remember. His long salt-and-pepper hair swings in front of his face as he struggles to get out of the cart, pop open his wheelchair, and settle in. As if Wylie Womack doesn't have enough problems with his crooked body, he also has emphysema. But Wylie doesn't let that slow him down. His motorized chair moves easily along the side of his cart.

I smell fresh coffee and look around, expecting to see Mom pouring some in Earline's cup. For a little person Mom sure leaves a big hole. If she wins the contest and gets a record deal, I guess Dad and I will have to blow this town and move to Nashville. Dad will rent the longest U-Haul trailer and pack up his worms, and we'll split down the road. Funny thing is, every time I try to picture Dad and me going to Nashville, Dad comes out like a blur in an overexposed photo.

Even though I know the menu by heart, I read the words over and over, trying not to think about Zachary Beaver over at the trailer or where Paulie Rankin went.

Ferris returns to take our order, and Cal asks, "Hey, any word on that freak show guy?"

"Haven't seen hide nor hair of him."

"Strangest fella," Earline says, overhearing our conversation.

"Where do you think he went?" I ask.

"Tobias," Dad says, his mind-your-own-business

tone attached. He's studying the menu and doesn't even look up when he says my name.

"Don't know," Ferris says. "It's got the best of me."

Earline looks up. "Whatever it is, it must be no good." She scoots her chair away from the table, causing it to screech. "I suspect the sheriff will be looking into it."

Miss Myrtie Mae sets down a saltine cracker and scowls at Earline. "A stranger can't spend five minutes in Antler without everybody suspecting he's a serial killer. Can they, Brother?"

The Judge doesn't answer. He stares in my direction; his dark beady eyes burn a hole right through me.

"Well," Earline says, walking out the door, "decent people don't leave a child unattended for days on end." She turns and looks at Miss Myrtie Mae. "Do they?"

Ignoring Earline, Miss Myrtie Mae picks up her cracker and takes a bite. Her mouth chews in exaggerated circles.

Ferris chuckles. "If Opalina had been here, she would make up a song about it. Probably something like 'The Ballad of Zachary Beaver.' "

Everyone laughs but Dad. He glances up from his menu. "I'll take a bowl of tomato soup."

Before going home, we buy a snow cone from Wylie

Wylie hasn't spoken in years, I guess on account of the emphysema. His cart is built low so that he can reach the ice machine and syrup bottles. Every Thursday the ice man delivers ice to the Bowl-a-Rama Cafe. Ferris lets Wylie keep the ice in his huge freezer since Wylie rents a room at the Sunset Motel and doesn't have a place to store it.

The colored bottles glisten in the sun. Grape, lemon, orange, watermelon, strawberry, bubble gum. They all look tempting, but as always, Cal and I order Bahama Mamas. While we suck the sweet red juice through our straws, I can't help thinking about Wayne. Cal must be too because before taking his first bite, he says, "Got a letter from Wayne today."

"How is your brother, Cal?" Dad asks.

"Fine. He sure misses home."

"I'll bet he does. Be good to have him back." A few years ago, Wayne helped Dad build the shelter for his worms in our backyard. Dad told him more than anyone would ever care to know about Tennessee brown nose fishing worms. I'm sure Wayne would have preferred talking about baseball or girls or anything besides worms. But Wayne would smile, nod, and ask Dad questions like he was really interested.

While Dad stops into the insurance office across the square, Cal and I eat our snow cones.

"Hey, watch this," Cal says, taking off for the trailer.

"Get back here!" My heart pounds in my ears. Wylie watches us, a blank expression on his face. I glance toward the insurance company. Dad's back side is to the trailer door.

Cal races up to the trailer, sets his half-eaten snow cone on the top step, knocks on the door, and runs back toward me.

"Cal, are you crazy?"

"Maybe he's thirsty."

We watch. Nothing happens. Even the wind is calm, as if it too is waiting. The cup sits on the top step, the red straw poking out of the snow cone.

Dad returns. "Ready, boys?"

We get into the truck and head home. But as we drive away, Wylie points in the direction of the trailer. We look and see a pale hand extend out the trailer door and grab the cup. Cal and I exchange glances but don't say a word.

It only takes a minute to reach home. Next door, Kate sits in the driver's seat of the station wagon, parked in front of their mailbox. She rolls down the window and holds up a small square piece of paper. "I got it! I got it!"

Dad thrusts his fist in the air. "That's great!"

I send her the thumbs-up sign, and even Cal calls out, "All right! Let's go for a ride."

Smiling, she waves, rolls up the window, and puts the car in reverse. And she's still smiling and waving as she hits the mailbox and it crashes on the asphalt.

While Dad rushes over to her, Cal shrugs and shakes his head. "Now I know what we can do with all those smashed-up garbage cans."

"What?" I ask.

"Make helmets for everybody in town. We're going to need them when Kate gets on the road."

Chapter Six

We can see all of Antler from the flat roof of the Bowl-a-Rama. We see the cotton fields and the cattle ranches stretched out beyond the town limits. We see hundreds of cars and trucks whizzing down the highway on their way to anywhere but here. And sky. We see lots and lots of sky. But today Cal and I have our eyes glued on one item—the grocery sack we just left on Zachary Beaver's trailer step. We lie bellies down on the roof and wait.

It's been three days since Paulie Rankin left, and we figure a big guy like Zachary must be running out of food. I brought tomatoes, butter beans, and onions from Dad's garden. Cal brought Twinkies, potato chips, and hot dogs.

Today I was the one who went to Zachary's door. I set down the sack, knocked, then ran across the street and climbed the Bowl-a-Rama ladder to the roof.

We watch the trailer door, but now we also watch anybody who passes or drives by. It amounts to Earline driving her Volkswagen to the courthouse, Malcolm and Mason going inside the Dairy Maid, and Miss Myrtie Mae heading over to the library, wearing her wide-brim straw hat.

"To protect her virgin skin," I say in my high-pitch imitation of Miss Myrtie Mae.

Cal hoots. "That ain't the only thing virgin about her." Cal's hand covers his heart. "Miss Myrtie Mae has a tragic past."

"How's that?" I ask.

"The fellas at the gin said when Miss Myrtie Mae was younger she was engaged to a lawyer from Wichita Falls. All her sisters had married and moved away. She and the Judge were left. Two nights before the wedding the Judge pretended to be on his deathbed. She postponed the wedding, but the lawyer broke up with her because he said she was already married."

"What did he mean by that?"

"He meant the Judge. The fellas at the gin say she was so dedicated to him, she would never have room for a real husband. After the lawyer broke up with her, the Judge made a remarkable recovery. Miss Myrtie Mae's only chance at love, and it was gone." Cal pretends to play a violin.

I don't like thinking of love and Miss Myrtie Mae in the same sentence. Especially since I seem to be as unlucky at it as she is. "Heard from Wayne?" I ask.

Cal sits up. "Almost forgot. I got another letter." He digs into his shorts pocket and reads it aloud.

Dear Cal,

Hope this letter finds you having a great week and that you are having the best summer ever. Have you had the Ladybug Waltz yet?

Our food supply has been low this week, so we haven't had as much to eat lately. Those chocolate bars Mom sent have sure come in handy. It's not that bad, though. Starting tomorrow, we'll have liberty for two days in Saigon, and I'm going to order the biggest meal I can find. After that, we'll be heading out, and I should see a lot more action. Remember when you, Billy, and me played war in the backyard? I guess I'll get to see it for real now. Don't worry about me. I've had a lot of practice throwing water balloons.

How is Mom? I'll bet her roses are really pretty this time of year. And I guess Dad is working as hard as always. Now, there's something I don't miss—hoeing that Johnson grass during the blistering heat.

Cal, I'd love to hear from you sometime. I guess you're like I was at your age, trying to crowd a lot of fun into every minute of summer before you have to go back to school. You and Toby have a blast on me, okay?

Your brother,
Wayne

"Did you write him back?" I ask.

Cal scratches the back of his neck. "Not yet."

I glance away. "You ought to write him."

"Hey, man, give me a break. I got the letter today. Besides, Kate writes him every day. I don't know what she has to write about. She's the most boring ugly person alive."

Time drags on. Our sweat attracts the flies from the Dumpster below, and our shirts stick to our backs. Out of nowhere Cal says, "Maybe Zachary is dead."

"Jeez, Cal!"

"Well, he hasn't answered the door."

"Maybe we should knock again."

But before we take off, the curtain in the trailer parts an inch.

We don't stir. We don't speak. We don't even breathe.

A moment later the door opens a crack, and though we can't see anything, we know Zachary Beaver is peeking through. The door swings open, and now we see all of Zachary as he bends down and lifts the grocery sack. He is huge. Bare chested, his gut tumbles out over his pants. His arms are rolls of dough, and his puffy bare feet peek out of his baggy pants legs. He struggles to stand, gripping the doorway to balance. And when he does stand, we see he has breasts like a woman. Even with the noise of the Bowl-a-Rama's air-conditioning unit, we hear him take a big breath before slamming the door.

"Whoa!" Cal says. "That's a whole lot of person. He could wear a bigger bra than flat-chested Kate."

I wonder what it would be like to be that fat. Once when I was nine or ten, Mom heard that a cold front might blow through the Panhandle. It was fifty degrees outside, but she made me wear a bulky sweater and my heavy winter coat. The cold front never arrived, and I felt like an enormous snowman, sweating under all those layers. I wonder if that's how Zachary feels every minute.

Mission is accomplished with the food delivered, and so we decide to go home.

"Go on without me," I tell Cal. "Dad asked me to stop at the Wag-a-Bag for milk and bread."

He starts for the ladder, jumps from the second step, and hops on his bike. At the bottom of the ladder, I notice he's dropped Wayne's letter. Since Cal is way down the road past the square, I tuck the letter into my pocket. I'll give it back to him later. But right now, for this short time, the letter is mine.

Chapter Seven

Four days have passed since Paulie Rankin left town. Today Cal and I place another sack of groceries on Zachary Beaver's steps. We've been here an hour, and he still hasn't opened the door. We wait and wait. I wonder if we wait to make sure he picks up the groceries or to get another glimpse of him.

At least today we came prepared, armed with a Sugar Daddy apiece, jawbreakers, and M&M's. Our teeth sticky from the caramel, we talk about Paulie Rankin. We even make up his history—where he was born and how he ended up as a sideshow owner. First we have Paulie figured out as a bank robber who uses Zachary Beaver to distract the law. Then we have him dodging a loan shark. Finally we decide he kidnapped Zachary and is hiding out from an orthodontist because of an unpaid bill.

While we wait, Malcolm's little brother, Mason, and four other chubby third graders show up with sticks in their hands. Unlike Malcolm, Mason is tough and the leader of his bully pack. Each kid takes a side of the trailer and starts hitting it with sticks. Over their pounding, Mason yells, "Hey, fat boy! Show your face!"

Something boils inside me. I remember when kids like them beat up on me just because they could. I wouldn't snitch, and since Dad was against it, I wouldn't fight back either. But today is different. Today we're soldiers, fighting for Zachary.

Thinking fast, Cal and I climb down the ladder and scoop up rocks from Ferris's rock pile out back. They're not big rocks, but from the roof they could sting the little brats' arms, backs, and behinds. Using our shirts as baskets, we carry the rocks to the roof.

Cal and I stand next to each other, our legs apart like camera tripods, our arms set in pitching positions. "Ready."

"Aim." I focus on Mason's butt.

"Fire." My rock sails through the air and hits a perfect target.

Mason's hands fly to his porky bottom. "Ow!" He looks up at the roof, shading his eyes with one hand.

When Cal hits Simon Davis's leg, Simon takes off crying, his hand pressed against his thigh. Cal trots in place. "And this little piggy went wee, wee, wee, all the way home!"

I throw again, this time aiming at James Rutherford's arm. I miss. Then I hear it. Glass breaking. The window shatters, and the boys scatter in different directions.

"Run!" yells Cal, and we do, leaving our bikes next to the ladder.

It's Thursday, and I wake up to the radio DJ yelling, "One more day until TGIF!"

Two things weigh heavy on my mind—Zachary's broken window and Mom's big night tonight. Nashville time is one hour ahead of us, but she's probably sleeping in. I picture her lying in a dark hotel room, eye mask covering her eyes, Dad's worn-out socks on her hands to lock in her Avon hand cream, and empty orange juice cans she uses for rollers crowded on her head. It's the best way, she says, to get big hair. I say it's the best way to get a big headache.

Since summer nights are usually cool in Antler, we sleep with the windows open and leave them that way until noon. But this morning the air conditioner is already running at full speed, so I get up and shut the window. Just as I'm about to flick the lock, I see the sheriff's car pull up in front. Sheriff Levi gets out and walks toward our house. Duke hangs his head out the window, his tongue draping from his mouth.

My stomach plunges. Zachary Beaver must have squealed. Maybe he saw us running away. Or it might have been nosy Earline, looking out her real estate office window. She has a full view of the trailer from her desk. I thought real estate agents answered the phone and showed homes to people, but Earline seems to do anything but that. Once I walked by her office window and found Earline with her feet propped up on the desk, painting her toenails. Cotton balls stuck between each toe.

From the living room Dad calls, "Toby!"

I feel sick. I yank on a pair of shorts and run downstairs. Sheriff Levi's arms are folded across his chest, and except for his usual eye twitch, his face looks blank. He pulls off his hat and rakes his fingers through his wavy hair.

I check out Dad's face, but it doesn't tell me anything except he hasn't shaved yet. "Toby, Sheriff Levi has something to ask you."

He's heard. Maybe I should confess. But Cal would get in trouble, and I'm not a snitch like Malcolm.

Sheriff Levi clears his throat, and his right eye twitches like crazy. "Toby, I have a favor to ask of you."

My stomach feels like a glob of lava in a lava lamp, slowly floating up toward my throat.

"Toby, reckon you and Cal could accompany me to that sideshow trailer?"

I don't know what to say. My knees shake, and the sheriff's eye twitches.

"Toby," Dad says, "the sheriff is asking you something."

"Sir?"

"I need to find out what those fellas' plans are, and since he's just a kid, I don't want to scare him or anything. Seeing a sheriff at your door can be intimidating. You know what I mean?"

He continues explaining. "Since you boys are about his age, maybe he'd relax a bit, open up and tell me the whereabouts of that other guy. The Dairy Maid has been mighty patient with them parked out front. Before he left, that sideshow fella paid them cash for the water and electricity hookup, but he said it would only be for a few days.

"Yesterday Ferris got an envelope in the mail from that guy with money for some meals for that boy. It had a San Francisco postmark, but no return address. Now the folks at the Dairy Maid want to know what's going on. Don't blame them one bit. And, well, it's my job to make sure strangers have a good reason for sticking around Antler."

Sheriff Levi doesn't mention the broken window. Bringing him straight to Zachary Beaver's door would be like asking me to pick out the electric chair for my own execution. Zachary probably assumes we broke it since he caught us peeking in it a few days ago.

"Tobias," Dad says, raising his eyebrow, "the sheriff is waiting for your answer."

I have no choice. "Yes, sir. Yes, sir, I'll be ready in a second."

Duke rides shotgun in the front while Cal and I ride in the backseat of the sheriff's car. I hold a sack of bell peppers and green onions Dad packed for me to give to Zachary. Cal acts like we're going on a field trip to Disneyland. I feel like I'm attending a funeral—mine. As we pull up in front of the trailer, I check out our bikes still leaning against the side of the Bowl-a-Rama.

Sheriff Levi parks his car and Cal bounces out. I take my time. As we walk up to the trailer, the sheriff looks toward the broken window, which is now covered with Wag-a-Bag grocery sacks. He tilts up his hat. "Wonder how that happened?"

After the sheriff knocks on Zachary's door, we wait

for Zachary to answer. When he doesn't, I'm thinking, Good, maybe we can leave. But Sheriff Levi knocks again and hollers, "Mr. Beaver, Sheriff Levi Fetterman here. I need a minute of your time, please."

The door slowly creaks open a few inches and Zachary peeks through with one eye. He huffs, beads of sweat rolling down his face like he ran the fifty-yard dash.

The sheriff clears his throat. "Mr. Beaver, sorry if I woke you, but I need to ask you a few questions. I brought along a couple of my young friends. This is Toby and Cal."

Zachary's eye narrows, and I know he remembers. I hold my breath, waiting for his finger to point our way. But he only nods and says, "We've met."

"Can we come in?" asks Sheriff Levi.

Zachary swings open the trailer door and we step inside. The smell of lemon Pledge makes me think back to the first day Zachary arrived. He's wearing a long red nightshirt like I saw in *The Night Before Christmas*. The ball of Zachary's right foot is wrapped loosely with gauze. Malcolm wears a size twelve, and Zachary's feet look a lot bigger. He wobbles across the room, the floor creaking with each step, and flops on the love seat, his bottom covering both cushions. He doesn't ask us to sit down, but there's no place to sit anyway. The Plexiglas panels rest next to the wall, folded like an Oriental screen. I see the fabric panel hanging at the other end of the trailer and wonder if the bathroom is behind it.

Sheriff Levi leans against an empty space on the wall. Cal looks around, his eyes casing out the place, and I can see his fingers itching to touch something. I take deep breaths through my nose and try to look relaxed. In one hand I hold the sack of vegetables, but I don't know what to do with my other hand. Finally I let it hang at my side.

Sheriff Levi glances around. "Nice little place you have here. You got about everything you need."

"It'll do," says Zachary.

The sheriff walks over to the window with the bags taped over it. "Looks like you have a problem with that window, though. Know anything about that?"

I hold my breath, concentrate on the floor, and prepare for the ax to fall.

Zachary stares at us, yawns, and locks his hands behind his head. "I guess some kids did it."

"Well, I'll drop by later with somebody who can fix that for you."

My heartbeat slows and my breathing returns to a regular pace now that I know Zachary doesn't have a clue it was us.

"Toby and Cal should be about your age," Sheriff Levi says. "How old are you fellas?"

"Thirteen," we say together.

"I'm fifteen," says Zachary, and the way he says it sounds like he thinks fifteen is as old as thirty.

"That a fact?" says the sheriff.

Zachary just stares.

Sheriff Levi folds his arms and clears his throat. "Mr. Beaver, you don't sound like a Texan."

"I'm from New York. New York City. Ever heard of it?"

Sheriff Levi grins. "Kind of a jokester, aren't you?" He looks down at Zachary's foot, and his smile drops into a frown. "What happened to your foot?"

Zachary covers his injured foot with his left one. "It's okay. I just stepped on a piece of glass."

The sheriff kneels in front of Zachary like a shoe salesman. "You better let me take a look at that."

"It's okay," Zachary snaps.

Sheriff Levi stands and steps back. "All right, but I'm sure the doctor at the clinic would be glad to take a look at it."

Zachary glares.

Sheriff Levi clears his throat. "Where is that other fella from? The young man you're traveling with?"

"Paulie? He's from Jersey."

"Is that where he is now?"

"No."

"Where is he, son?"

"He's looking for another act to add to our show, but I don't know where he is."

Zachary frowns at Cal, who is lifting the lid off the gold box. "Put it down. My mom gave that to me."

Cal lifts a black book out of the box. "It's just a Bible."

"It's not *just* a Bible. My mom gave it to me when I got baptized."

Cal flips to the front pages.

"Cal, put the boy's Bible down," Sheriff Levi says in a gentle tone. Cal slaps the Bible shut and returns it to the box.

I'm wondering why Levi Fetterman ever became sheriff. He's too soft, and I can tell he hates asking these questions by the way his eye twitches and he keeps clearing his throat.

"Where are your parents?" Sheriff Levi asks.

"Rosemont Cemetery."

"How's that?"

"Dead."

Sheriff Levi clears his throat, and his eye looks like it's going to take off. "Sorry about that, son. Life can be tough."

"I'm not your son," Zachary says.

The sheriff swallows. "Well, of course not. Sorry. Didn't mean to offend you. Who is your legal guardian?"

"Paulie Rankin's my guardian."

Sheriff Levi grimaces, and his voice becomes firm. "I see. Well, I hate to break this to you, Mr. Beaver, but if Mr. Rankin doesn't return in a week, I'm going to have to take some sort of action. I really should be doing it now. This isn't a campground, and the court would view you as a minor who has been left unsupervised and abandoned."

"Paulie will be back. He always comes back."

"How do you know?" the sheriff asks.

"I'm his bread and butter."

Sheriff Levi looks at Zachary with pity, and I wonder if he's thinking about taking him home like one of his adopted dogs. "How is your food supply?"

"Fine. As you can see, I'm not starving."

Sheriff Levi turns to leave. "Well, you fellas stay and get acquainted. Maybe you could invite Zachary to pal around with you." I try to picture Zachary riding a bike or climbing on top of the Bowl-a-Rama, but the bike tires flatten and the ladder steps to the roof break.

The sheriff's hand rests on the doorknob. "Mr.

Beaver, you enjoy your stay in Antler. But I hope your friend returns by the end of next week. I truly hope he does. And one more thing, you can expect a visit from the doctor about that foot."

The sheriff leaves, and Zachary smirks at the closed door. "Oooh, he's got me shaking in my boots."

I want to tell him how lucky he is that the sheriff hasn't hauled his butt off to New York City. Instead I hold out the sack of bell peppers and green onions to Zachary. "I brought you some vegetables. They're from my dad's garden."

"The refrigerator is behind you," Zachary says. In Antler it's considered rude to order people around and not even say thank you for a gift, but I remember his parents are dead. If I were an orphan, I probably wouldn't have any manners.

I expect an empty refrigerator, but it's stocked with food. Among the eggs, cheese, and milk is a Bowl-a-Rama barbecue plate and a Chicken Delight casserole covered in plastic wrapping. Ferris must have already visited Zachary, and there is only one person in Antler who makes Chicken Delight casserole—Miss Myrtie Mae Pruitt. Just when I think there isn't anything I don't know about boring Antler, something happens and takes me by surprise.

Zachary sneezes so loud, it sounds like the roof could cave in. "It sure gets dusty here quick," he says.

"It's the wind," I explain. "It blows all the time."

Zachary points to the light fixture. "Could you dust that? I hurt my back picking up the glass."

"No sweat," Cal says since he's the only one who can reach it. A second later Zachary has me dusting the end table. He's bossy and grumpy, and if I didn't give it any thought earlier, I've decided I don't much like Zachary Beaver. But the dusting is the least I can do, considering I broke the window.

Cal dusts the lower bookshelf while trying to take a peek at the albums. "I can reach *that*," Zachary snaps.

With a shrug, Cal leaves the cloth on the shelf. "Hey, this is neat." He grabs a book titled *Sideshows*.

"That's Paulie's," Zachary growls. "Put it back."

Slowly Cal returns the book to the shelf. "Are you in there?"

"Nope."

"Who's in there?"

"A bunch of old acts. Most of the people are dead or retired. But one day I'll be in a book."

"How's that?" I ask, thinking about what Cal and I discovered at the library.

"One day Paulie and I will both be in a book

because we're going to have the biggest sideshow business ever."

I force a laugh. "You mean the smallest. You're only one act."

"Not for long," Zachary says. Maybe Paulie Rankin is really out drumming up more business. Maybe he's looking for a two-headed person or a turtle man.

"Who usually does the cleaning for you?" I ask.

"Paulie. What do you cowboys do around here for fun?"

"We're not cowboys," I snap, wondering why I'm helping this guy who thinks he's such a big shot.

"Isn't this Texas, where the buffalos roam and the deer and the antelope play?"

I throw down the dust rag. "Not everybody in Texas has a ranch."

"What do your parents do, then?"

Cal flops on the floor. "My dad grows cotton. Toby's dad is the postmaster, but he also raises worms."

My ears burn.

Zachary laughs. "Worms?"

"Yeah, worms," I say. "It's not like he travels around in a trailer and charges people to look at him or anything."

I expect him to snap back, but he rubs his chin. "And what do people do with *worms*?"

My mouth opens, and I repeat all the things Dad has ever bored me with about worms. "Worms are being used in Florida to help break down landfills, and their soil makes some of the richest fertilizer on the earth. Cal's mom uses it on her roses, and she grows some of the best in Antl—in Texas. And—"

"Mostly people use them for fishing," says Cal. I want to bust his lip. I know I'm trying to make my dad sound as important as the United States president.

"Some French people eat worms," Zachary says.

"I know that," I say, but really I've never heard of anything more ridiculous.

"You like to shoot cans?" Cal asks.

"Shoot cans? Is that what you do around here for fun?"

"Well, what do *you* do for fun, besides watching TV and reading?" I ask him.

Zachary smirks. "Nothing around here. But I've done plenty."

"Like what?" I ask, and the way he meets my gaze, he knows I'm challenging him.

"Like ride the elevator to the top of the Eiffel Tower and cross the London Bridge and look out from the top of Seattle's Space Needle."

When we leave, Zachary adds, "Oh, don't forget your bikes. You left them by the Bowl-a-Rama yesterday."

Outside the trailer, I ask Cal why Zachary didn't squeal on us.

"Maybe he has a few secrets of his own."

"What do you mean?" I ask.

"Well, for one thing—Paulie Rankin. I think Zachary knows where he's at. And we already know he's probably not the fattest boy in the world. And then there's that Bible. He said his mom gave it to him when he was baptized."

"So?"

"Iola Beaver, I guess that's his mom, gave him the Bible. Her name is in there, but the baptism information is blank. If you're given a Bible when you're baptized, wouldn't that be the first blank you filled in? It doesn't make sense."

And for once, Cal does.

Chapter Eight

"She didn't win." Dad says the words at dinner like he's asking me to pass the salt.

Although I feel a twinge of disappointment for Mom because I know how much she wanted to win, I'm relieved. "Then she'll be coming home tomorrow?"

Dad stirs his peas into the mashed potatoes on his plate. He's getting pretty good at cooking vegetables, but his mashed potatoes are lumpy. And of course, there's no gravy.

"She'll be staying on awhile."

"What do you mean? If she lost, why is she staying?"

"She got runner-up, and apparently some hotshot manager in the audience thinks he can get her a record deal."

Suddenly nothing on my plate looks good. "How long will that take?"

Dad finally looks at me. "Those kind of things can take a long time, Toby."

"How long?"

He looks me square in the eyes. "Sometimes they never happen."

"Well, Mom wouldn't stay forever. How long will she stay?" I'm almost yelling.

"Toby, I'm not the person to answer that question. I'll give you her phone number and you can ask her yourself."

"Yeah. Give me the number. I'll call her."

Dad shakes his head, gets up, and goes into the kitchen. The way he walks with his jaw set and shoulders stiff reminds me of something I had forgotten or blocked out. *The fight.* Their last fight. It was in this room. At this table. Dad got up and stomped away, angry, while Mom continued to yell at the wall. Shutting my eyes tight, I try to erase that memory, but it plays over and over in my mind. And the strangest thing is I don't even remember what the argument was about.

Dad stands in front of me, a piece of paper in his hand.

I take it, push my chair away from the table, and run up the stairs. I grab the hall phone with the long extension, take it into my room, and stretch out on my bed. I start to dial the number, then stop. I don't need to talk to Mom. She won't stay away long. She wouldn't. After all, she didn't take her old guitar and pearl necklace. She would have taken them for sure if she wasn't coming back.

And if Mom does get a record deal, she'll send for me in a heartbeat. We'll travel around the country in her big bus that says Opalina Wilson and the Delta Boys or whatever her backup group is. I'll count her money for her. I'll be her manager. I'll be the youngest manager in the history of country music. Probably in the history of any kind of music. The Delta Boys will call me Tex. I close my eyes and watch the tail end of that big bus ride down Interstate 40 to towns where people crowd into concert arenas to hear Mom. My breaths even out with each billboard we pass.

When I wake up, the clock on my nightstand reads ten minutes past ten, and for a minute I don't know if it's the same night or the next day. Outside my window, stars twinkle in a dark sky. I've been asleep for three hours. The pants I wore yesterday are slung across my chair, and Cal's letter from Wayne is poking out of the back pocket. I forgot to return it to Cal today, but he never mentioned losing it. Goofy Cal probably doesn't even know he dropped it yet.

I get up, pull out the letter, and read it again and again. Then I tear a piece of paper from last year's math notebook and write a letter to Wayne. I tell him all the things Cal and I are doing. I tell him about Kate getting her driver's license, his mom's roses, and Zachary Beaver coming to town. I tell him that the ladybugs haven't arrived yet and that we ate Bahama Mama snow cones at Wylie Womack's stand and thought of him. I tell him all these things and more. And then I sign—*Sincerely, your brother, Cal.*

A few minutes pass, and I hear Dad snoring down the hall. Holding my shoes, I walk down the stairs and try to keep the steps from creaking. Outside, I get on my bike and ride to the mailbox in front of the post office before heading to the lake. It's cool, and the breeze feels good against my face. I open my mouth, wishing I could swallow enough air to lift me like a hot-air balloon and carry me away from this stinking town.

At the lake I jump off my bike, run up to the water, and lie sprawled flat on the grass, looking up at the millions of stars and the full moon. The moon reminds me of times when I was five or six and couldn't fall asleep. Mom would slip into my bed next to me and shine the flashlight on the dark ceiling.

"See the moon," she'd say, pointing to the perfect round light. "Let's make it dance." She'd move the flashlight, causing our moon to trot or waltz back and forth across the ceiling. We'd laugh, and she'd make that moon dance until my eyes got so drowsy, I fell asleep. Of course, that was kid stuff. These days I lull myself to sleep thinking of Scarlett swinging back and forth on her porch swing.

Music softly plays, and I figure it's from some house far away, but the sound gets closer. James Taylor is singing "You've Got a Friend."

"Are you okay?" Scarlett stands above me, holding a transistor radio. I look at her red toenails and wonder if she puts cotton balls between each one before painting them.

Most guys would jump up, but I lie there like a dork and squeak, "Yeah, I'm fine." I don't know what it is about this girl that makes my voice go up two octaves.

"Are you sure?" From the ground, I have an incredible view of her long legs wearing a pair of short white cutoffs. Now is a good time to get up, but I stay there, stretched out on the ground like some corpse. "Yeah, kind of tired. Rough day at the office." My ears are on fire. All the words in Webster's dictionary and I choose those.

Finally I sit up. "Do you come here often?" I ask. Each second I approach dork eternity. But she doesn't seem to notice.

"Not that often. Only when I break up with a guy."

"You broke up with Juan?" I try not to sound too excited, but my words come out squeaky. If I stay calm, I'll have this voice thing under control. Though it's hard to stay calm.

"Yeah, looks that way." Her voice quivers, and she chews on a long strand of hair. She's just inches from me. I want to reach for her, pull her toward me, and tell her it will be all right. I want to smooth her hair, massage her neck, kiss her toes. Instead I wrap my arms around my knees.

"Why'd you break up?"

"He stood me up. He said he'd go with me to my great-grandfather's birthday in Amarillo. We gave him a big fancy party for turning eighty."

"Man, that's old."

Scarlett sits next to me. A shiver runs through my body. "For two months Juan kept saying he was going. Then at the last minute, he backed out. He didn't even give me a good reason."

"What a jerk," I say in a deep voice.

"Do you have a cold?" she asks.

I skip a rock across the water, thankful that it's dark because my face feels red.

I'm feeling guilty for all the things I'm thinking about, but I know I would be in heaven just holding Scarlett Stalling's hand.

We sit there together in silence, listening to the music from her transistor radio.

"I love this song," she says, turning up the volume. "Close to You" by the Carpenters plays, and I bob my head to the music, wishing I had enough nerve to ask her to dance. If I only knew how to dance, I probably would.

"Would you dance with me?" she asks.

"Sure." I stand, feet planted firmly on the ground, arms glued to my sides.

She giggles. "It would help if you put your arms around me."

A huge lump slides down my throat. I circle her shoulders, wishing I had taken a Fred Astaire class or something. Wherever people learn to dance. Once Mom tried to teach me the two-step in the kitchen, but I was a complete klutz.

Scarlett pushes my arms lower until they surround

her waist. Her hands lock together behind my neck, and she starts to move slowly in a circle. I follow her lead.

Even standing in bare feet, she's a few inches taller than me. My forehead tingles from barely touching her chin. Her skin is smooth as powder. I try to breathe in her scent, but I suddenly become aware of my sweat. If I knew I would have ever had a chance at dancing with Scarlett Stalling at Gossimer Lake tonight, I would have worn deodorant. I would have rolled a whole bottle over my entire body. Because just the sight of Scarlett Stalling makes me sweat. And now being this close to her, I'm sweating buckets.

"This is nice," she says. The way she says that in her sweet voice makes me remember to breathe. And in this moment I actually enjoy dancing with her to that song. Heck, we *are* that song. *Why do stars fall down from the sky every time you walk by? Just like me, they long to be close to you.*

"Ouch!" She releases me and jumps back.

"Did I step on your toes?"

"No." She slaps her arm. "Mosquitoes! When are they ever going to spray around Antler?"

Suddenly I feel them biting my ears, my cheeks, every inch of my exposed skin.

"I better go," she says. "Thanks for the dance, Toby.

You're great!" She leans over, kisses me on the cheek, picks up her radio, and dashes off.

I'm great. Me, Toby Wilson. Great. She said it. She even sealed it with a kiss. Or did she say it's late? No, she said *great.* I ride back home with Scarlett Stalling's kiss on my cheek, thinking how Wayne is right. Antler is the best place on the face of the earth.

Chapter Nine

I decide to mow the Pruitts' yard early because these days the temperature hits ninety degrees by noon. And I plan to spend the afternoon claiming the left side of Scarlett's swing.

The smell of fresh coffee drifts up to my bedroom. When I make my way downstairs, I'm surprised to see Dad at the kitchen table in his T-shirt and plaid pajama bottoms. Usually he's dressed for work by now. His hair sticks up and out like a mad scientist, and dark half-moons lurk below his eyes like he hasn't gotten a wink of sleep.

"Morning," he says, rolling the rubber band off the newspaper.

"Morning," I say, shuffling into the kitchen.

This is my first day at a real job—a job that has nothing to do with worms. I figure that deserves some sort of initiation. I pour coffee in Mom's Grand Ole Opry mug. Suddenly I feel numb, and it dawns on me why Dad looks lousy. Dancing with Scarlett clouded my thoughts, and I had forgotten about Mom—until now.

When I sit at the table, a small smile pulls at the corners of Dad's lips. "When did you start drinking coffee?"

I shrug, sort of embarrassed. "I don't know. This morning."

He picks up the sugar bowl. "Sugar?"

"Nah," I say.

He watches, waiting for me to sip. When I don't, he looks down at the newspaper. I lift the cup and take a big swallow. It burns.

Glancing at me over the paper, Dad smirks, then clears his throat and frowns, looking back at the paper as if he didn't notice me gagging. A moment later he says, "Do me a favor. Take that bucket of soil on the back porch over to Gloria. And give her that sack of tomatoes on the counter too."

Dad must feel rotten. Mrs. McKnight is one of the few people he enjoys talking to. She likes hearing about the optimum temperature for worms, and he likes learning about the different types of roses.

In Cal's backyard, Mrs. McKnight hangs underwear on the clothesline. Mom says Charlie McKnight is too stingy to fork out enough money for a clothes dryer. Every member of the McKnight family is represented on that line except Wayne. There's Cal's small Fruit of the Loom underwear, Billy's larger ones, and Mr. McKnight's boxers. Next to them hang pink polka-dotted and solid blue panties. Mrs. McKnight grabs a red bra from the plastic laundry basket and clips it to the line. I'm wondering if the bra is hers or Kate's when she peeks around the boxers and notices me staring at the bra. My whole body blushes.

Smiling, she says, "Oh, Toby, I didn't see you standing there."

I try to speak, but the words stick in my throat like cotton balls. All I can say is, "Err . . . uhh. Uhh—"

She glances down at the bucket. "Did your dad send me some of that terrific soil?" I think it's funny how people who like growing things call dirt "soil."

"Uhhh, yeah. Yes, ma'am."

She walks up to me and takes the bucket. "Thanks. I'll return your bucket later."

I hold out the sack, and she accepts it.

"These too?" She puts down the bucket and looks inside the sack. After taking a long whiff, she smiles. "Aaah. Fresh tomatoes. What a good neighbor. Tell your dad thank you for me." She takes a few steps, then stops. "My gracious, I almost forgot. How did your mother do last night?"

I'm not ready to explain because I'd have to confess I don't know when Mom will be back. "The Grand Ole Opry had a fire, and they postponed the contest."

"Oh, my goodness. Did anyone get hurt?"

"Oh, no, it only burned in the part where they were going to hold the contest."

Her forehead wrinkles. "Oh. Oh, well, I see."

"They haven't rescheduled it yet. Mom's hanging around till it's over."

Mrs. McKnight's smile makes my stomach knot up. "Well, wish her the best of luck for me when you speak to her."

I take off for the garage and wonder why I lied to Mrs. McKnight. She's the nicest person I've ever known, and I lied to her as easy as I did to my math teacher when I told him I forgot my homework. Only this lie makes me feel worse.

Miss Myrtie Mae's house is around the corner from ours on Cottonwood Street, so I don't have to drag the lawn mower very far. The Pruitt home is the biggest house in Antler. It stands green and tall behind two huge willow trees. Their house is the first one Cal and

I hit on our Halloween route. Every year Miss Myrtie Mae dresses like Glinda, the good witch in *The Wizard of Oz*, and gives out candy bars from the front porch. Her wrinkled face is a scary sight under that curly blond wig and rhinestone tiara, but it's worth looking at her and putting up with her Glinda speech in exchange for an Almond Joy.

Today Miss Myrtie Mae greets me at the door and tells me to wait in the living room with the Judge while she gets her list. I'm hoping it's short because of my big plans this afternoon at Scarlett's house.

The Judge sits there, fumbling with his pocket watch. Before Miss Myrtie Mae leaves the room, she says, "Brother, you remember Tobias Wilson, Opalina's boy? I'll be right back, Toby."

The Judge looks up, and stares at me. His head is cocked sideways and a string of drool hangs from the corner of his mouth.

Everything in the living room is either green or gold. Last year Miss Myrtie Mae hired a decorator from Amarillo to do over the entire house. Miss Myrtie Mae accidentally left the decorator's bill out when Miss Gladys Toodle was visiting. Ten thousand dollars. It was the talk of Antler until Christmas, when Miss Myrtie Mae and Miss Toodle competed with their outdoor decorations. They used so many outdoor lights, the entire town lost its electricity for a day.

Old black-and-white photos in silver frames crowd a round oak table near the couch. One is of two boys about my age in old-fashioned baseball uniforms. Another is of a pretty girl with a bow in her long dark curls. I figure they must be from the good-looking side of Miss Myrtie Mae's family.

I'm taking a closer look at the photos when the Judge says, "Young man."

I turn. He squints at me. "This is the last time I want to see you in this courtroom."

Glancing around, I realize he must be talking to me. "Judge, I think—"

He shakes his finger at me and the string of drool has grown longer, stretching past his chin. "Don't talk, son, when I'm handing down a verdict. I'm tired of this nonsense. Now you're going to have to do some time instead of paying a fine."

The front door is six feet behind me and I'm tempted to escape this crazy old man, but I've got a girl now, and I'll earn more money today than Dad has ever paid me.

The Judge stands, leaning heavy on his cane. "Young man, do you understand me?"

He inches toward me. I back toward the hall

and duck my head around the corner. "Uh, Miss Myrtie Mae?"

She returns, and it's the first time in my life I have been happy to see Miss Myrtie Mae Pruitt. The sight of the Judge breathing down my face doesn't fluster her at all. She pulls out a wadded tissue from her pocket and wipes his drool.

"Brother, this is Toby. He's our new lawn boy. Remember early this summer we had that nice McKnight boy, William? And I know you remember Wayne before that." She turns to me. "Brother loved Wayne. That youngest boy, though. He filled in for Billy once last year, and my heavens, you never saw such a mess—patches of tall grass, weeds left in the flower beds." She clicks her tongue. "We couldn't have that."

I feel bad for Cal. Maybe he *knew* the reason Miss Myrtie Mae didn't ask him to mow her yard this summer.

Miss Myrtie Mae hands me the list. Twenty-three tasks are marked on it, and I wonder how I'm ever going to see Scarlett before the sun sets.

"Come on," Miss Myrtie Mae says with a quick wave of her hand. Her pointed navy blue shoes tap against the wood floor.

I follow her into the backyard. As I scope out the grass carpet spread to eternity, I realize that the Pruitts not only have the largest house in Antler but they also have the biggest lawn. Morning glories spill over the back fence. A stone path winds its way to a white gazebo big enough for a high school band. Two apple trees' branches droop, heavy with apples, and the fruit litters the ground beneath them. I glance at the list.

#1: Pick up apples off the ground.

Miss Myrtie Mae points out the beds that need weeding. "Now, if you're ever in doubt if it's a weed or not, give me a holler. Better safe than sorry. I'll be in my darkroom." She leaves me alone in the yard.

Every green apple I pick up has a hole in it. I can't get away from worms. The vinegar smell of rotting apples on the ground makes me want to puke, and roly-polies invade the fruit like an army climbing over green mountains.

#2: Mow lawn in an east-west pattern.

The yard seems to go on forever. East to west. West to east. The mower roars and spits grass blades to the side. The smell of freshly cut grass fills the air. Halfway through the job, I decide mowing isn't boring if you make your own designs. I make a circle, a square, then a triangle. Nothing to it, so I move on to more complicated forms. I zigzag along the fence. I make curlicues. I begin to spell Scarlett. I—see Miss Myrtie Mae peeking out her window, frowning at me. I stop in the middle of my letter *S*. East to west. West to east.

About the time I finish mowing, Miss Myrtie Mae comes outside, carrying a silver tray with a glass pitcher of iced tea, some lemon drop cookies, and jiggly lime Jell-O stuff. She must think we're going to have a tea party. Sheriff Levi follows her, his head and shoulders drooping, like a kid ordered to go to church. Seeing him makes me think about Zachary, and I wonder what the sheriff will do if Paulie Rankin doesn't return.

"I reckon you deserve a break by now," Miss Myrtie Mae says. Her bun is loose, and wiry gray strands stick out around her face. "Sheriff Levi happened by at the right time."

Sheriff Levi wears a pair of plaid shorts, a yellow knit shirt, and his lucky fishing hat decorated with tackle. "Well, actually, Miss Myrtie Mae, I just came by to ask Toby something." I'm willing to bet he wants worms.

Miss Myrtie Mae acts like she can't hear him and

proceeds down the stone path. "Let's sit in the gazebo, where there is plenty of shade."

She sits in the white rocker and motions the sheriff and me to the chairs around the wicker table. I collapse in one of them, but Sheriff Levi keeps standing. He glances at his watch, and his eye twitches. "Miss Myrtie Mae, this must be such an inconvenience, me barging in on you and all. I really just want to get some—"

"Nonsense!" Miss Myrtie Mae says. "Now sit!"

"Worms," he says as his rear end meets the chair.

"It's too hot to eat anything warm, so I made my lime gelatin turkey salad." She slices a piece of the wiggly stuff onto a china plate and hands it to me. My stomach feels queasy at the sight of turkey chunks floating inside lime Jell-O. I glance at Sheriff Levi, and the way his eye twitches studying the Jell-O, I figure he feels the same way.

I'm sweaty and not sure Miss Myrtie Mae would approve of me using her nice fancy napkin to wipe the sweat from my forehead. I don't know what to do with that napkin, and I watch Sheriff Levi, but he doesn't seem to know either. So I wait for Miss Myrtie Mae's cue. She flings hers open and drops it daintily into her lap. The sheriff and I follow her lead, only when

I fling my napkin, one corner lands in the pitcher of iced tea. I go to rescue it, only to knock my glass of ice over.

"Whoa, whoa, Toby," she says. "Sit back. I'll get you a clean glass of ice." I want to tell her don't bother. I'm filthy and sweaty, and dirty ice won't hurt me at this point. In fact, any kind of ice sounds great, but she swiftly removes the glass and disappears into her house.

Sheriff Levi leans over the table and whispers fast, "Toby, can I help myself to some worms? I'm heading out to my secret fishing hole."

"Sure, Sheriff, help yourself."

"I'll leave the money in the tin can."

"No problem." Dad leaves an empty coffee can on the shelf so the locals can take what they need and leave the money in case we're not there, but Sheriff Levi always hunts us down before taking any.

Miss Myrtie Mae heads our way with my glass of ice, so I quickly ask, "Sheriff, what could happen to Zachary Beaver if Paulie Rankin doesn't come back?"

Sheriff Levi tips back his hat. "I'll have to notify social services in Amarillo."

"What does that mean?"

He tries to steady his eye by raising his brows. He removes his hat and wipes the sweat off his forehead with a handkerchief. "He'll probably be put in a foster home or some sort of home for juveniles."

"Oh." I look away. Some blurry white moths fly by, their wings fluttering in the breeze. I don't like Zachary Beaver, but I don't much like the thought of him living in some house with strangers either.

Miss Myrtie Mae hands me the fresh glass of ice. "Here you go, Toby."

Sheriff Levi shovels the salad into his mouth in quick huge bites, then washes it down with iced tea, holding his head back as he empties the glass. Giant gulps move down his throat, then he stands and announces, "Miss Myrtie Mae, I hate to eat and run, but I forgot Duke was waiting for me in the car." He grabs a couple of lemon drop cookies, tips his hat, and steps off the gazebo before Miss Myrtie Mae can utter a protest.

Four hours later I sack up the grass, then cross off task number twenty-three. The flower beds are groomed and free of weeds. I feel proud. I'm different than Cal—I finish projects. I remember when Cal and I were five or six and we turned on the garden hose and made a mess in the mud. Wayne fetched Cal and cleaned him from head to toe with the hose before taking him into the house. I cleaned myself off. I don't have big brothers watching out for me.

Before paying me, Miss Myrtie Mae inspects the yard. She walks to each corner flower bed. Her eyes comb every grass blade, and when she spots an apple on the ground, she walks over and picks it up. It probably fell a second ago.

She hands me my money and says in a sharp voice, "Not bad, but next time take care in the direction you mow. You shock the grass blades if you don't cut it in an east-to-west pattern. Can I expect you next week?"

My arms ache from pushing the lawn mower, my back throbs from bending over picking up apples, and my hands have blisters on them from pulling weeds. I open my mouth and say, "Yes, ma'am."

Miss Myrtie Mae asks me to step inside the house for a moment, and I'm relieved that the Judge isn't inside, waiting to haul me off to prison. Smells of something wonderful drift from the kitchen. The TV is on, and the early evening news broadcasts from a jungle in Vietnam. I wonder if Wayne is nearby.

Miss Myrtie Mae shakes her head, looking at the television. "Oh, that mess! I hope you never have to see war, Toby. Our poor Wayne. I include him in my prayers each and every night." She looks up at me like she has just thought of another list of chores for me to do. "Toby, almost forgot about your mom. How'd she shake out?"

I don't even hesitate. "The place where they were going to hold the contest had a fire, so they—"

Her eyebrows shoot up. "The Grand Ole Opry burned down?"

"Uh, it was only a small fire, but they postponed the contest. She's waiting around until they reschedule it." I'm turning into a full-fledged pathological liar.

Miss Myrtie Mae lowers her eyebrows and frowns. I study the rug covering her wood floor. "That a fact?" she asks. "Hold on. I'll be right back." She walks into the kitchen, and I wonder if she's calling Dad to check if I'm telling the truth. But a moment later she returns with a pan covered with aluminum foil. "Would you mind taking this German chocolate cake over to Mr. Beaver's place? He mentioned a fondness for chocolate."

I leave with the pan, wondering how I'll manage to get it and the lawn mower home without dropping it. I also wonder how much daylight is left before my plans to see Scarlett sink fast below the horizon. As soon as I clean up, I'm going straight to Scarlett's. Mr. Zachary Beaver will have to wait for his cake.

As I reach the bottom step of the Pruitts' front porch, I hear a creak. "Stop right there, young man."

I swirl around. The Judge leans forward in a porch rocker, shaking his cane at me. "You remember what I said, you hear?"

Chapter Ten

Tired to the bone, I arrive home around five o'clock and head for the shower. Mom used to nag me about washing places like my elbows or the back of my neck. Not today. When I step out of the shower, my skin feels raw from scrubbing every inch.

A towel wrapped around me, I lean into the mirror and examine my upper lip. Fuzz. I wonder if whiskers are like pimples and that one morning I'll wake up with a face covered with them. I splash on some of Dad's Royal Copenhagen aftershave. And today I use deodorant.

Before leaving, I stick a note on the refrigerator with a magnet telling Dad I'll be home for dinner. Then I take off for Scarlett's house.

All the homes on Scarlett's street look pretty much alike—tiny with single garages and small yards surrounded by link fences. But one has a wooden porch swing with the left side reserved for me.

At Scarlett's house I hide the German chocolate cake between a bush and the fence. Since Miss Myrtie Mae covered the top with aluminum foil, it should be safe until I take it over to Zachary.

Scarlett is exactly as I pictured her, sitting on the porch, her long legs stretched across the swing. A magazine rests in her lap, and she's so engrossed in it, she doesn't see me.

Before I step through the gate, Tara and three other little kids march past me in a line. Upside-down plastic plant pots perch on top of their heads. Tara, the leader of the pack, has about seven vacation Bible school ribbons pinned to her shirt. Moist wisps of hair cling to her sunburned face.

She walks up to me and says, "We're having a parade, and I'm the mayor. And they're the Shiners." This kid grows weirder by the minute.

"You mean *Shriners*," I say.

"That's what I said. Shiners."

I ignore the brat and slow my pace toward Scarlett. No reason to seem too eager. It spoils the image. Scarlett is thumbing through her magazine, popping her chewing gum, and doesn't notice me until I step onto the porch. She looks up and smiles, her lips shiny with lip gloss. "Hey. How ya doing?"

Oxygen leaves my body in one big *whoosh.* "Fine."

I remember to breathe again, only I suck up too much air and start coughing. I cover my mouth and try to swallow, but it's no use.

"You okay?" she asks. "Do you need a glass of water?"

Holding up my palm, I manage to say, "I'm fine." I wish I could start all over—opening the gate, repeating my slow cool walk toward the porch, maybe a casual lift of my eyebrows when she says hi.

But Scarlett doesn't seem to mind. Her gaze slides over the magazine page and she sighs. "You know, there's a whole world out there waiting in the back of magazines."

"Hmm? You mean in the ads?"

"Yeah. Didn't you ever want anything in the back of a magazine?"

"Well, I always wanted to order those sea monkeys in the Superman comics. But my dad said they were a waste of money."

She laughs. "Sea monkeys?"

I feel my face go red. I decide not to mention the Atlas Body Building course.

"I mean these kind of ads." She points to an ad

about a modeling school in Dallas right next to one about becoming a stewardess. The wind blows her hair across her face, and a few strands stick to her lip gloss. She swings her feet to the porch floor and scoots over, leaving room for me on the right. It's not the left, where Juan sat, but I guess it really doesn't matter.

Leaving a foot of space between us, I sit next to her and take deep breaths. Her hair smells like flowers.

I want to hold Scarlett's hand, but mine are sweaty. I should have used deodorant on them. Maybe one day I'll invent a hand deodorant and market it to guys like me who want to get rid of their wet palms.

"Is that what you want to be?" I ask. "A model?"

"Maybe, if I can get these fixed." She taps on her two front teeth.

"What's wrong with your smile?" I know she's talking about the gap, but I love her gap.

She sighs. "Oh, Toby. You have to be perfect to be a model. And I'd look better without it. See?" She smiles, and a piece of chewing gum fills the space.

I shrug.

"Or maybe a stewardess. That would be the next best thing, to fly around the world. How glamorous."

I'd ridden in a plane once when we flew to my grandmother's funeral. The stewardesses served drinks, handed out peanuts, and asked if we had any garbage. A little kid threw up on one of them. But I decide not to mention any of that.

She tucks a strand of hair behind her ear. "Of course, to be an international stewardess, I'd have to know another language." She says *international stewardess* like it's as official as a U.S. ambassador job. "Juan was helping me learn Spanish before . . ." She gazes into the yard.

I should have listened to Dad and enrolled in Spanish class last year instead of shop. He told me learning a foreign language would come in handy. Just as I start to scooch toward her, Scarlett stands, stretching her arms above her head. "I've got to cook dinner. Mom will be home from work any minute. You can come in if you want."

If I want? Yes, I want. I follow her into her house, which is dark and smells musty like an attic. Clothes cover shabby furniture and toys litter the floor. Scarlett breezes into the kitchen, dodging the whole mess. I stub my toe on a giant baby doll with batches of hair torn out.

Scarlett fills a pot with water. "Toby, would you get my radio? It's in my room."

I glance around for a door.

"Go down the hall. It's the first door on the right."

In the room, two unmade twin beds have matching floral bedspreads, but it's as if there is an imaginary line drawn down the middle of the floor. One side has a ton of stuffed animals and dolls without arms and heads. I swear Tara is headed for the women's penitentiary.

The other side of the room has Bobby Sherman posters taped on every square inch of the wall. I remember signing the Autograph Hound sitting at the head of her bed. It was the last day of school. I should have written something great like *Peace* or *Stay cool.* But I signed, *See you next year, Toby Wilson.*

I walk over to her dresser and pick up a cologne bottle. Wind Song. My hands shake, but I remove the cap anyway and smell it. The smell is faint, so I spray a little on my hand and take a close sniff.

"Ummm!" Tara stands in the doorway, the plant

pot gone from her head. "Scarlett, Toby's spraying your perfume!"

I put down the bottle, grab the radio off her dresser, and head out. My face burns, and I know the scent gives me away.

Scarlett drops pasta in the water while I wipe my hand on my jeans.

With hands on her hips, Tara says, "Toby tried your perfume."

Shaking my head, I talk fast. "I knocked the bottle over when I grabbed the radio. Then the top fell off and I put it back."

"Na-ah!" Tara says. "You sprayed on some perfume!"

"Oh, Tara," Scarlett says. "Scram."

The phone rings and Scarlett lunges for it, picking up the receiver before it finishes the first ring. There's no denying it. This girl has answered many phone calls.

"What do you want?" she says into the phone. "It's Juan," she mouths.

Tara pulls at my shirt. "I want to see him again."

Ignoring Tara, I try to hear Scarlett's every word and not look interested. I watch the pot of water boil.

Scarlett sighs. "I don't want to talk to you." She sounds cold, almost mean, but I'm thinking, Yeah, cool, she doesn't want to talk to you.

Tara tugs at my shirt again. "I want to see *him*!"

"I have company," Scarlett tells Juan.

Yeah, Juan, I think, go lick your wounds. She's got a new man.

"Who?" Scarlett glances my way.

I swallow.

"Toby Wilson."

Why did she have to say that? My stomach dribbles like a basketball. I see Juan towering over me with his number-five iron. I should have sent off for that Atlas Body Building course.

"Don't call back." Scarlett hangs up the phone. She bites her lower lip and tears fill her eyes.

"What's wrong?" I ask, reaching for her arm.

But Scarlett steps away from my touch, shakes her head, fumbles through a drawer, and grabs a can opener. "Nothing."

It doesn't matter. I already know. It's the words she's etched all over her notebooks since fifth grade—*Scarlett Stalling loves Juan Garcia.*

Tara stomps her feet. "I WANT TO SEE THE FAT MAN AGAIN!"

"Tara, stop screaming!" yells Scarlett. She sighs, and her voice softens. "Toby, would you mind?"

"No," I lie. "Not at all." I leave the girl of my dreams in the kitchen, pining over some other guy, while I take her possessed sister to see Zachary Beaver. Loser is my middle name.

Chapter Eleven

The foil is missing from the pan of German chocolate cake and flies swarm around the icing. I hunt around for the foil, thinking maybe it flew off in a gust of wind. Something shimmers on Tara's wrist—a bracelet made of aluminum foil. She sees me looking and quickly hides her arm behind her back.

I snap. "You took the foil!"

"We need to be shiny. Shiners are suppose to be shiny."

It's no use now. I pick up the cake, inspect it for damage, and decide it looks okay. Except for the flies. I swat them away, but not before they land on the sweet icing and rub their legs together, celebrating their good luck.

"I'm surprised you didn't eat the cake."

Tara frowns and plants her hands on her hips. Her

fingernails wear chips of the same red as Scarlett's toenails. "My momma says it's not nice to steal!"

Cal's bike is parked in front of Zachary's trailer. I'm wondering why he didn't tell me he was coming here, then suddenly I remember the letter to Wayne. I feel sick. Before knocking at the door, I turn and tell Tara, "You can't stay long. Only one minute. No, make that one *second*."

Cal answers the door. "Where have you been? I went by your house, but you weren't there." He tugs at one of Tara's ponytails. "Hey, squirt!"

Tara doesn't say a word. She just stands frozen in the doorway, mouth open, eyes wide, staring at Zachary.

Zachary stares back, then fills his mouth with air, puffing out his cheeks.

Tara screams, squeezes past me, and rushes out the door. "He's blowing up! The fat man is blowing up!" She screams all the way across the parking lot, past Wylie Womack's stand on the square, and we still hear her scream after she disappears around the Bowl-a-Rama toward home. I want to shake Zachary's hand. Instead I laugh. Cal does too, and now even Zachary smiles.

Finally we calm down, and we're quiet for a long

moment as the wind howls outside the trailer. Cal stretches out on the floor, his chin resting on his palm.

Zachary wrinkles his nose. "What's that I smell?"

I hold out the pan. "Miss Myrtie Mae's German chocolate cake. She sent it over for you."

"Not that. The perfume."

My face burns as I remember my close call to victory.

"Nothing."

"You smell like a French prostitute."

"Do you want the cake or not?"

"Well, slice it, Cowboy," Zachary says.

"Yeah, Cowboy," says Cal, smirking. "Get that chow served."

I frown at Cal.

Zachary tells me where he keeps the knife and the plates. A minute later, I'm serving the cake like some cook on a cattle drive. While I put the cake on the plates, I notice the new window. "Who fixed it?"

"The sheriff," Zachary says. "What a goofball. Does his eye always do that?"

"All the time," Cal says.

I look down at Zachary's foot. The loose gauze covering has been replaced by a tighter fit. I figure the sheriff must have sent the doctor like he said he would.

Zachary stares at the piece of cake I hand him, his face scrunched up. "What? No forks?" I'm happy using my hands, but I traipse over to the kitchen drawer and dig out a fork for Zachary and Cal. Zachary takes it and says, "The napkins are over the sink."

I turn to give Cal a fork and napkin, but he licks his fingers and announces, "I'm through." Sure enough, not a crumb is left on his plate.

I don't care for Miss Myrtie Mae's fancy salads that jiggle, but she can bake better than anybody in Antler. I love the rich icing best, mixed with its tiny pieces of pecans.

Zachary snarls as I devour my slice, using my fingers. "You guys are pigs."

"Yep," says Cal, then he belches.

When Zachary asks for another piece, I say, "Get it yourself. I'm not your mom." Then I remember. I am a loser and a sucker and an insensitive pig.

"How did your mom die anyway?" Cal asks.

Zachary ignores him. He grunts, raising himself from his seat, and wobbles to the other side of the trailer. I feel the floor move and pray the trailer won't tilt.

Cal waits for Zachary to answer, and when he doesn't, Cal tells me, "Heard about the fire at the Grand Ole Opry."

My stomach feels queasy.

"A fire at the Grand Ole Opry?" Zachary asks. "I didn't see anything about it on the news."

"It was just a small fire," I say, and this time I almost believe it. But the way Zachary stares at me, with one eyebrow lifted, I think he knows it's not true.

Cal wipes crumbs off his mouth. "When do you think your mom will be back?"

I shrug and say, "I don't know."

Zachary returns to his seat with an enormous piece of cake. I guess he figures, What the heck? We know he didn't get fat eating carrot sticks. "Where is your mom?"

"Nashville."

"Trying out for a singing contest," Cal adds.

"What does she sing?" Zachary asks. "Hillbilly music?"

"Yep," Cal says.

I glare at him. "No, she doesn't. Country music. You know, like Tammy Wynette."

Zachary looks like he's about to laugh. "Is that her name?"

"No. My mom's name is Opalina Wilson."

Zachary snorts, and I want to cram that giant piece of cake down his throat.

Cal stretches on the floor again, tucking his hands behind his neck. "Tell us more about Paris."

Zachary tells us about visiting the Louvre. "It has 350 rooms."

He sounds like an encyclopedia. I yawn, doing my best to act bored. Zachary Beaver is full of it.

"How did you climb the stairs?" I ask.

We lock eyes, and he says, "I used the elevator. Ever seen one of those?"

"Doesn't it have a weight limit?" I ask.

"Very funny, Cowboy." He turns to Cal, who is hanging on every word.

I'm grouchy and feeling mean. I should be eating spaghetti at Scarlett's house or at least some meal that Mom cooked. Instead, I'm eating German chocolate cake in a dark, cramped trailer.

Cal sits up and out of the blue asks, "Did you get baptized in France?"

Zachary frowns. "Why do you want to know so much about my baptism?"

"Well," Cal says, "you never got around to having the minister fill out your baptism information in the Bible."

"I didn't say I got baptized. I said I *almost* got baptized."

Cal and I look at each other. We know what we heard.

"How does someone *almost* get baptized?" I ask.

Zachary stares at me a long moment before saying, "I'm getting tired of answering you country idiots' dumb questions."

Jumping to my feet, I say, "Don't bother. I'm leaving anyway. See ya!" I slam the door on the way out.

Cal catches up with me as I reach the Bowl-a-Rama. "Why'd you have to get him mad?"

"If you want to stick around and let him make fun of you, go ahead."

"Ah, he doesn't mean anything by it. He's just lonely."

"Oh, wow, Cal. That's a hard one to figure out. He's staying by himself in a trailer in the middle of Nowhere, Texas." Suddenly what Sheriff Levi told me at Miss Myrtie Mae's house about juvenile hall comes back to me, and I feel a twinge of guilt.

At home, a letter is lying on my bed. It has a Nashville address and it's postmarked Tuesday. That means Mom wrote it before the contest. I rip it open.

Dear Toby,

The contest is in a couple of days, and I'm as nervous as a mouse in a cat kennel. But when I'm onstage at the Grand Ole Opry and the lights shine down on me, I'll be fine. Heck, it'll be all I can do to keep myself from bending down and kissing the stage. Imagine me, Opalina Wilson, standing in the very spot as Tammy Wynette, Loretta Lynn, and Conway Twitty. Mercy! It'll be like standing on holy ground.

Critter, what I'm about to write is pretty darn hard for me. And I'm writing it before the contest because I wanted you to know this has nothing to do with whether I win or not. Me and your dad have been having a rough time of it lately. You've heard us arguing. Or I guess you've heard me hollering and seen your dad stomping off. I guess I need some time to figure everything out.

And don't you go blaming yourself. You're

the best son a mother could have. I'm not leaving you, Critter. Your dad has my phone number, and I'm only a dime away. Come to think of it, that would be a good title for a song—"Only a Dime Away from Your Love." I know this will take some getting used to. Please don't hate me. It would tear my heart to shreds. I'll write you soon with my new address.

Love always,
Mom

I rip the letter into confetti, then throw the pieces out the window.

Chapter Twelve

It's the second Saturday of the month, and that means worm day—the day I help Dad box up and deliver worms to the bait shops around the lakes. To Dad, it's another exciting day with worms. To me, it means getting up before dawn.

Mom always fixed pancakes on the day we made deliveries. She'd say, "You need a breakfast that will stick to your ribs." As if boxing up worms and driving from bait shop to bait shop was hard manual labor. I'd give anything to have a stack of those golden cakes with maple syrup dripping over them. Since Mom left, I've woken up starving because Dad's suppers are heavy on vegetables and light on meat. They slide right through, leaving me hungry ten minutes later.

Downstairs the house is dark, except for the yellow glow from the hood light over the stove, where Dad stands, frying spatula in hand. A lopsided stack of pancakes sits on the table.

Dad looks up, kind of grinning. "I'm starting to get the hang of this. Don't worry about eating the ones on the table. These are going to be better."

I head toward the pantry. "I just want cereal." I don't even have to look to know he's disappointed, and for some reason I feel satisfied knowing that I've hurt him.

Later at the table, Dad reads the paper while I try to hike my eyelids enough to see the spoon to my mouth. I focus on the Elvis plate hanging on the wall. Mom bought that two summers ago, when we went to Memphis on vacation. It hangs between the North Carolina plate and the Florida one. I don't know what Elvis has in common with Florida and North Carolina, but Mom says he balances out the wall.

Outside the sky is pitch-black, and the air feels unstirred because the wind hasn't picked up yet. From a distance I hear the moan of the train passing through town. Light slips underneath the shelter's door because Dad keeps it on over the worms at all times. If he doesn't and it starts storming, the worms will split, heading for the hills or wherever worms escape.

The boxes line the shelf with labels that tell us the dates we last changed the soil. Some have *Separated* marked on them, meaning we've sorted them by age. Dad thinks it's amazing that in three months a white threadlike worm develops into a four-inch worm with a pale ring around it. I think Dad needs to get out in the real world more.

Dad hands me a tower of round cartons. "We'll need about a hundred boxes this morning."

I know the procedure. Fill boxes with peat moss. Dig for a worm. Worm in box. Repeat twelve times. Lid on. Next box. Dad always gives a baker's dozen—thirteen to a box.

I guess to most people it would feel creepy to fumble through warm dirt, feeling hundreds of worms wiggling against their skin. And it's not my favorite thing to do, but I've gotten used to it. After all, I'm Toby Wilson, son of worm man.

Dad flicks on the cassette player he keeps on the top shelf. Classical music bounces off the tin walls. Mom wrote a song about Dad digging for worms while listening to Beethoven. It's called "Wolfgang Wiggle."

The packing takes us an hour, and we let the piano sonatas fill the quiet. Maybe Mom would have stayed if Dad did something more interesting than raise worms and work at the post office. But it probably wouldn't matter anyway. She wanted to be a singer ever since I remember. I wonder if she wanted to be one when she was my age, like Scarlett wanting to be a model or a stewardess. Maybe living in a place like Antler makes people latch on to big dreams instead of drying up and blowing away.

Finally we pile the cartons into the truck and head east to the bait shop on Lake Kiezer. At Claude, we turn off the highway and onto the road that winds through Palo Duro Canyon. The canyon breaks begin about a mile out of Claude. They seem to rise out of nowhere and then suddenly the land flattens again.

We cross at the Prairie Dog Town Fork of the Red River, only it's nothing but red mud today. Dad shakes his head. "I don't know how the ranchers and farmers are making it this year, dry as it's been."

"Cal said Mr. Boggis lost his cotton crop."

"Makes a man glad he's raising worms."

I wonder if he's being funny, because it sounds funny, but Dad isn't the type to joke. I check out his face. He's serious. "You know, Charlie McKnight may be tight with his money, but it's probably what's saved his farm over the lean years."

"Why did you leave Dallas?" I ask. Dad's never given me a straight answer when I've asked before. In Dallas, my uncle and aunt are lawyers in my grandfather's firm. They drive nice cars and live in big fancy houses.

The creases dig deeper into Dad's face, but he keeps his eyes fixed on the road. "There's nothing in Dallas worth staying for."

I've heard that answer other times, before, but today I want more. "What about your family?"

"My family is here."

"Mom isn't here."

Dad is quiet for a moment, then says, "You read her letter?"

A lump gathers in my throat, and I can't speak. Outside the window, tall sunflowers along the road wave to us. Mom loves sunflowers. She once told me, "Being a farm kid, I grew up despising them. And then on our first date, your dad stood at my door with a silly grin on his face and a jelly jar of those weeds." Over the years sunflowers became her favorite. Dad used to give them to her on their anniversary, but now when I think about it, I can't remember the last time he did.

"I read the letter."

We're quiet again, and I wonder if this is what our life is going to be like from now on. Big empty spaces of silence like the wide-open land spread on both sides of the road.

I decide not to let my question die. "What about Uncle Arnie and Aunt Maureen?"

"What about them?"

"Didn't you ever want to be a lawyer like them?"

"Nope."

"Didn't you ever want to—"

"Toby, I like my life. Your mother didn't like hers, and that's why she isn't here. And when you grow up, you can decide where and what your life will be."

I feel trapped, but I don't know where I would go if I could leave. I wouldn't go to Nashville like Mom because everybody there probably wants to be a country music star. I wouldn't want to live in Dallas because it's not far enough away from Antler to feel like you've really been anywhere. And I wouldn't want to travel in a trailer like Zachary Beaver, never having a place to call home. I only know that now with Mom gone, the only thing keeping me in Antler is an impossible dream. Heck, I know I'll probably never see *Scarlett Stalling loves Toby Wilson* scribbled across her notebook, but there's something inside me that won't let go. If there was ever a chance that she could be mine, it's now, while Juan is out of the picture.

The sun starts to rise as we reach the marina. Inside the shop, the smell of coffee dripping mixes with a faint fish odor. Freddy, the bait shop owner, is setting out ketchup bottles on the counter in the eating area. As usual, a yellow baseball hat covers his bald head and red suspenders hold up his baggy pants. "How are ya?" he asks. "Toby, you look like you just rolled out of bed. Got some fresh coffee, Otto."

"Sounds good," says Dad. "We'll get these boxes unloaded for you first. Toby, you think you're up for a cup of coffee?" He winks, but I don't say anything. Dad acts like everything is the same this morning, when it's not.

After we unload the cartons, I swig down a bottle of Coke and look at the pictures of people and the fish they caught posted on the bulletin board. The weight of the catch is scribbled underneath each photo.

Dad sits at the counter, drinking a cup of coffee, while Fred points out a picture of the biggest bass that was caught yesterday. "Five and a half pounds."

"Not too shabby," Dad says.

"Hate to tell you this, Otto, but he caught it with one of those night crawlers."

"That a fact?"

"Of course I have to order those from Canada, so there's no tellin' when I can get them. They aren't as handy as getting hold of you and your Tennessee brown nose babies. The young man who caught that bass got back from Vietnam last month. Won't hardly speak to anyone. His dad said, when he landed in San

Francisco, he stepped off the plane and was spit on by hippies. You believe that? After serving our country. Damnedest thing."

"Damnedest war," Dad says.

Freddy clears his throat. "Yeah, well, I was in World War II. Back then, we came back heroes."

Dad doesn't say anything, and the quiet is so uncomfortable that I keep staring at the pictures on the board. But all I can think about is how Wayne *is* a hero and how no one better ever spit on him.

After a long moment Freddy asks, "You like to fish, Toby?"

I shrug. "It's okay."

Dad holds the coffee mug close to his chin. "I think my son has a dose of big city in him."

"I didn't know you ever lived in the city, Toby."

I frown because I know what Dad is referring to, and I don't see how asking a few questions about why he left Dallas makes me a city kid.

Dad takes a sip of coffee, then says, "He kind of thinks cities like Dallas have something special."

I'm wondering why Dad, who is private about everything, is talking like this to Freddy.

"Oh, they do," Freddy says. "Yes, indeedy, they do. They got traffic jams, and smog, and oh, yeah, they got those big ol' shopping malls where you can spend every bit of your hard-earned money."

My blood boils, and when we get back into the truck, I'm quiet. I don't even ask to stop at Prairie Dog Fork on the way to the next shop. And when Dad slows down anyway and asks if I want to see the prairie dogs, I say, "Nah."

Without saying a word, he accelerates, and I add, "Prairie dogs are no big deal."

He shrugs, and I say, "If you've seen one prairie dog, you've seen them all." It's no use. Dad is as good at the silent treatment as I am. Mom would be chattering away right now, saying something about the sunflowers blooming early or pointing out a family cemetery in the middle of nowhere. She always got us to talking again, mainly to shut her up.

Maybe Mom *will* make it big and I'll be a famous country music star's kid. I'll enroll at my new school in Nashville, and the teachers will say, "This is Tex Wilson, Opalina Wilson's son. No, he doesn't have time to sign autographs. Just treat him like anybody else." Only the kids won't because I'm Tex Wilson, number-one son of a top recording star.

I'll drive a Jag to school. I'll even parallel park it out front. I'll have my own wing in our mansion next door to Tammy Wynette. She and Mom will be best friends. They'll roll each other's hair on those giant orange juice cans. I might even date Tammy Wynette's daughter. And poor Scarlett. Poor, poor Scarlett. She'll write to me, and I'll dictate letters to my personal secretary that will always end with, *I'm sorry that Antler drives you crazy. Maybe I'll send my limo down to pick you up this summer. Then again—maybe I won't.*

"Toby?" Dad stands beside the truck, looking at me through the passenger's window. Somehow we've made it to the lake, and we're parked in front of Bob's Bait Shop. "Are you ready to unload?"

There's nothing like worms to bring you back to reality.

Chapter Thirteen

More than half the days in July are crossed off my calendar. Wayne will return in 224 days. Cal hasn't mentioned another letter from Wayne, so I figure he doesn't know about the one I wrote yet.

Today Cal and I stand on my unmade bed, throwing darts at the dartboard on the wall. Paulie Rankin left eight days ago, and Cal can't stop talking about Zachary Beaver and thinking of ways to get him out of the trailer. Now he wants to take Zachary to the Sands drive-in theater.

I aim toward the bull's-eye and miss. "Zachary will never go for it."

"Sure, he will."

"Cal, he's not going to go to the drive-in with us. For starters, how's he going to fit in a car?"

"We'll take the pickup. He can ride in back."

"And how is he going to get into the back of the truck?"

"Haven't figured that out yet." Cal jumps off the bed. "Hey, how about a ramp?"

"He's too heavy. He'd never make it down without falling."

Cal gathers the darts on the board and picks a couple off the dresser. "Are you playing with these soldiers?" He holds one up.

"Nah, I just had them out." I yank the soldier out of his hand and put it back on the dresser.

Cal shrugs. "We could back the truck up to Zachary's door."

"It's too low." I don't know why I'm talking about it. I don't want to go anywhere with Zachary. He's grumpy and rude and I don't like him. I grab a dart that Cal missed off the dresser and discover another letter from Mom. Dad must have placed it there last night. I'm not opening this one. I don't want to hear her claim she hasn't left me when she lives thousands of miles away. I try to forget about her by concentrating on the dartboard. It doesn't work. So I decide to join Cal in planning a way to get Zachary in the truck.

"We gotta think of something," Cal says.

My dart hits the center. "Bull's-eye!" Sinking to the floor, I try to sound bored with the whole matter. "We could make some steps for him. Dad's got wood out in the back that he's been keeping forever."

Cal grins, holding up his hand. "Good idea!"

Without enthusiasm, I slap his palm. "But even if we make the steps, who's going to drive us?"

Cal hunches his shoulders and begins singing "You Make Me Feel Like a Natural Woman."

"No!"

"It's the only way!"

"No, Cal. Not Kate."

"Why not?"

"For one thing, I'd like to live to see my fourteenth birthday."

"Oh, come on. She's got her license. And as long as she doesn't have to parallel park."

"Forget it."

Cal slumps to the floor, acting like a kicked dog.

"All right," I say. "But time's running out. We better start making the steps now. And we still have to convince Kate." *And Zachary Beaver.*

After measuring the distance from the ground to the back of the pickup, we grab Dad's tools and start to work. An average person wouldn't need to have wide steps, but we triple the width for Zachary. We don't need any accidents waiting to happen.

Halfway through the job I say, "You sure Kate's going to go for this?"

"It's not like she has a date or anything."

He's right. When other girls Kate's age started going to the movies with guys, Kate stayed home. She made some of her friends' prom dresses, but she didn't go.

I always liked shop, and it feels good to make something with my hands. I love the smell of freshly cut wood and how smooth the grain feels after going over it with sandpaper.

The afternoon sun beats down on us as we work, and we sweat enough to fill a bucket. After banging our thumbs with a hammer a couple of times, we decide to make sure we aren't doing this for nothing.

At the McKnights' kitchen table, Kate is busy sewing. The sound track of *My Fair Lady* plays from the stereo. She's wearing bell-bottom jeans and a blue knit top, the same kind of clothes that Scarlett wears. Only they don't do for Kate what they do for Scarlett.

When we ask Kate about taking us, she stares at Cal and me like we asked her to drive the getaway car in a bank robbery. "Absolutely not! If you think I'm going to have any part in making fun of that poor boy, you're dead wrong."

"We're not making fun of him," I tell her.

"Yeah, right." Her foot stomps the sewing machine foot pedal, and the needle races over the fabric.

"We're not, Kate. Honest." Cal sounds sincere.

Kate ignores him, her head bent over the sewing machine, as she sings with the song on the stereo. "I could have danced all night! I could have danced all night!"

"Oh, come on, Toby," Cal says, yanking at my shirt. "Let's forget it. Some people are too important to help out a lonely guy. Zachary will probably have to go to juvenile hall any day now."

We turn and move slowly toward the door. Kate stops singing. "What are you talking about?"

Together we face her, but this time I speak. "The sheriff said if Paulie Rankin didn't come back by the end of the week Zachary would have to go to juvenile hall or a foster home."

"Come on, Toby." I follow Cal out of the house and into my backyard.

I know what's going to happen next. If I had a million dollars, I'd bet it. We slowly pick up the tools. The McKnights' sliding glass door opens, and out of the corner of my eye I see Kate's lanky shadow on her porch. I wink at Cal and say, "Yeah, I guess we might as well stop making these steps."

Cal knows she's there too because he shouts, "Yeah, no use making anything for Zachary. What a waste, man."

I'm afraid he's overdone it, but Kate pokes her head over the link fence, her glasses resting on top of her head. "Are you really making those steps for him?"

We look up, trying to act surprised, and together say, "Yeah."

"And you aren't going to be mean to him?"

Cal rolls his eyes like he'd never think of such a thing. "No, Kate."

She checks her watch. "There's a John Wayne movie that starts at eight-thirty. Can you finish those steps by seven-thirty?"

"You bet," I say. "I got an A in shop last year."

"Me too," adds Cal.

"Your *only* A!" she says before disappearing into the house.

A couple of hours later, we finish making the steps. But we still have our biggest task ahead—convincing Zachary.

~

Cal and I decide not to ask Zachary ahead of time. If we show up ready to go, maybe he'll feel more pressure. Of course, we don't tell that to Kate; she'd never go for it.

At eight we load the steps into the back of the pickup and head toward Zachary's. As we get closer, light from the setting sun bounces off the yellow trailer, casting a haze around it like something in a dream.

Kate pulls up in front of the trailer and slams on the brakes. Our bodies jerk forward, and we nearly hit our heads on the dashboard.

"Sorry about that," she says. Before Cal can make a wisecrack, I nudge him in the ribs.

"Ow! What was that for?"

"Stay here, Kate," I say. "We'll be back soon."

We knock and, as usual, we wait.

"Let's bring up the subject slowly," I say. Cal nods. Finally the doorknob turns. Zachary's hair sticks up on one side like he's been sleeping. Inside the trailer is dark, and the TV blares from the corner.

Cal blurts out, "We came by to take you to the drive-in theater."

Zachary frowns. "I'm not going anywhere."

"Have you ever been to a drive-in?" I ask.

"No, Cowboy. Why would I want to do that?"

"It's another thing you can add to your list of adventures," Cal says.

"Yeah," I say, "when you're talking to people about the Eiffel Tower in Paris or being at the top of the Statue of Liberty in New York, now you can add seeing a drive-in movie in Texas. Besides, you've been wanting to see a cowboy. Here's your chance. It's a John Wayne movie."

Zachary snorts.

Since I figure he's too embarrassed to admit he can't fit into a car, I say, "We brought the truck. We can all ride in the back."

"We even made steps for you," Cal says.

Zachary's eyes grow wide, then quickly narrow. I wonder if he thinks we're up to something, so I part the curtains. Kate has managed to get the steps out by herself and put them in place. "See."

Zachary leans to look out the window. "You shouldn't have bothered."

There's a knock at the door. *Great.* One more minute and I would have convinced him.

From behind the door, Kate calls out, "Cal, we better hurry."

"Just a minute," Cal calls back.

"Is there a problem?" she asks.

"Who's that?" asks Zachary.

There's only one thing left to try. I head to the door and open it. "Kate, meet Zachary. Zachary, Kate."

"Hi." Kate holds out her hand, smiling. Her eyes soft, she looks at Zachary like she's seeing something more than fat. And for a second, the way Kate stands there with her hand out, smiling, she almost looks pretty.

Zachary stares at Kate's hand, and I just know he's going to snub her. But he accepts it, shakes, and smiles. A really big smile. It's the first time I've seen his teeth. They are perfect—white and straight. No gaps. Scarlett would be jealous.

"You ready?" Kate asks.

"Yeah," Zachary says. "Give me a second." He wobbles to the back of the trailer and disappears behind the drape. We hear water running and a minute later he returns, his hair wet down and combed.

To get through the front door, Zachary must squeeze sideways. He makes me think of Winnie-the-Pooh getting stuck in Rabbit's hole. But Zachary's belly presses against the door frame, and he jiggles his way through. Even though the sun is setting, Zachary squints and shadows his eyes with his hand. I guess he hasn't been outside in weeks. Maybe months.

Even though Kate parked close to the trailer, Zachary takes a while to make it up the steps. As he moves, the fat beneath his loose shirt causes the fabric to ripple. Each step, he stops and rests. Drops of sweat cover his upper lip, and he pants like a Saint Bernard after a run. Finally he makes it to the bed of the pickup. He lands with a loud thump, and we feel the bed move. Cal and I have to step over his legs because there is no way he can scoot to the front.

"How's the foot?" I ask.

"Fine," Zachary says. He looks around, taking in the world through narrowed eyes.

The road is empty except for us. We pass a farm with a tractor left out in the field, and in the distance a dust whirlwind blows near a ranch house. And even though my bruised thumb still throbs from hitting it, the cool breeze feels crisp smacking my face and I'm feeling good because of what we're doing for Zachary.

After a few minutes Zachary says, "It reminds me of the sea."

"What?" I ask.

"The plains. It's like an ocean. See." He points to a windmill standing against the sunset. "There's a lighthouse. And look at the rows of cotton. When you pass them, they look like waves."

"You think?" Cal asks, his eyes scoping the cotton fields.

"I don't see it," I say.

Zachary smirks. "You don't know how to look. You have to really look at something."

I've looked at cotton fields all my life and never once did they remind me of an ocean.

A couple of miles outside of Antler, more cars appear. Kate drives as slow as a little old lady and people honk or pass us, shaking their fists. A carload of older kids ride by, their window rolled down. Two of the jerks hang out, making obscene gestures and yelling, "Lard butt!" We look like we're hauling Buddha across Texas. Suddenly I'm kind of wishing that I hadn't listened to Cal and I hadn't suggested making the steps.

Zachary stares at the side of the road. I wonder how he visited all those places he claims he has. How did he fit in the elevator at the Louvre? How did he handle the stares and the insults?

At the drive-in's entrance, Kate stops the truck to pay the ticket guy. "Hey, Billy's sister, right? You can go in free."

"You sure that's okay?" Kate asks.

"Sure." He smiles, flashing his braces, and waves her on in. He doesn't see Zachary at first, but his chin drops as the back of the pickup passes him—it nearly hits the ground.

Zachary notices and quickly turns away. He presses his arms against his sides and folds his hands in front of him like he's trying to make himself smaller.

Only a few other cars have arrived, but Kate parks the truck in the back row. She probably did that so no one would park behind us and bother Zachary. She climbs out and motions to Cal. "Let's go get some drinks and popcorn."

I want to yell, Don't leave me alone with *him*. But Cal hops out and follows Kate to the concession stand. It would be rude to follow and leave Zachary alone. But I want to. Man, I want to. Sitting back here in the truck with him, I feel like *I* am Zachary Beaver. I see the glares and fingers aimed our way. I hear the fat jokes. This must be what it's like for him when he's traveling around the world. Then it hits me hard. Zachary hasn't gone to all those places. From the way he diverts his eyes and draws up in himself, I doubt Zachary ever leaves his trailer.

To avoid the stares, I study the giant screen. I watch kids swing at the playground in front. I count the speakers in the first row. Around us crickets chirp, car engines cut off, and voices scatter into the night. We listen, but we don't speak.

Finally Zachary says, "So this is a drive-in theater?"

"Yep, this is it, all right. Nothing much."

We're quiet again, and I figure I should say something. "You ever go to the movies?" I feel like punching myself. How could he go to a movie? He couldn't fit in a seat.

"Yeah, all the time."

Zachary is a big liar. Then I remember. The entire town thinks the Grand Ole Opry burned down. I'm just thankful Dad is a hermit because I'd be grounded for life if he caught word of it. It's probably only a matter of time.

Kate and Cal show up just as I think of something to say. Kate climbs into the back with us and hands Zachary a Coke. She points out the speakers and tells him how, when she was younger, their family piled into the station wagon and came to the drive-in. The kids wore their pajamas and took their pillows. And their mom always brought a paper sack full of popcorn.

"Really? Cool," Zachary says, nodding. He acts like Kate said she flew to the moon in a rocket that she sewed on her sewing machine. Zachary seems different than usual—nice. And he's not eating any popcorn. Cal and I stuff the buttered kernels in our mouths. We were so busy trying to finish the steps that we hardly ate any dinner.

Kate sips her drink through a straw. "I understand your mom died two years ago. That means you were only thirteen, right?" The way she asks doesn't sound mean or nosy at all.

"Yeah."

"Was she fat too?" Cal asks. I should slug him, but Kate does it instead.

Zachary looks at Kate when he answers. "She was a big lady. Big heart too. Went to church all the time."

Leaning back against the cab, Kate gently asks, "Is it hard having people walk through your home looking at you?"

"Well," Zachary says, then pauses. "They're going to stare anyway. I might as well get paid for it." He looks deep into Kate's face. "Pretty soon the money will be even better because Paulie and I are adding some acts to the show. That's what he's doing now."

"Why didn't he take you with him?" Kate asks.

"He had to go far away. It was easier for me to stay here." He quickly glances at us. "This time."

Kate nods like she understands Zachary's crazy world. As we wait for the movie to begin, Kate talks to Zachary. Zachary talks to Kate. And it's as if we're not sitting in the back of a pickup with the fattest boy in the world. It's as if we're alone on a boat in the middle of an ocean—a prairie ocean—eating popcorn and sipping sodas, listening to Zachary tell us more about his real life. I say real life because somehow I can tell the difference with this talk and the stories about France and England and Seattle. And I can't help wondering if *my* lie is as obvious to others.

"Did you go to church with your mom?" Cal asks,

and I know where he's heading. Cal is going to die from curiosity about that baptism.

Music begins to play, and the movie starts. Zachary never answers.

Cal's shoulders slump, and he clicks his tongue against the roof of his mouth. "Jeez!"

I'm disappointed too. Then I wonder why *I'm* now interested in Zachary's baptism story.

As soon as the movie ends, Kate turns the ignition key and pulls out before the credits start to roll. I guess she wants to leave before Zachary gathers more attention.

After we drop Zachary off, Cal whispers, "I have an idea."

"What?" I ask.

"I think we should help Zachary get baptized."

Chapter Fourteen

Two days after the movie, Cal and I are on the roof of the Bowl-a-Rama. It's seven o'clock in the evening, but the summer sun hasn't set. It sits in the sky like a bright juicy orange waiting to drop from a branch. These are the longest days of the year.

"You should know how to get baptized," Cal says.

"Why me?"

"You're a Baptist."

"Well, I've never been baptized."

"I'm a Catholic," Cal says. "We get baptized when we're babies, and Zachary's a long way from being a baby. You'll have to find out."

It's true. Mom and I went to church every week, and at least once a month I watched Reverend Newton dunk someone in the baptistery. I'd seen simple-minded Kirby Waddel go under at least a dozen times.

He thought he needed to be cleansed every time he cussed or sassed his mother.

I haven't been back to church since Mom left. And Dad doesn't make me because, except for funerals, he never goes.

Cal looks like he's waiting for me to say I'll find out. "What makes you think he wants to be baptized anyway?" I ask.

"Think about it. His mom gave him a Bible for his baptism. He admits he *almost* got baptized. And his mom is dead. She probably died before it happened. Maybe it was her last wish."

"Jeez, Cal. You've got some imagination." I want to shrug it off, but the weirdest thing happens. Kate pulls the truck in front of the trailer, gets out with a stack of books, and knocks at the door. Zachary peeks out the window and eventually opens the door. A few moments later Kate leaves with a grocery sack.

"What do you think is in it?" Cal asks.

"Heck if I know." But I'm dying of curiosity too. The only sacks I've seen pass Zachary's steps are going in, not coming out.

Later Cal calls me on the phone. "Want to see what was in the sack? Meet me in my backyard."

Out back, Cal stands in front of the clothesline, his

arms spread wide. It takes a second to register, but then I see. A gigantic pair of pants, two shirts, and several of the biggest boxer shorts I've ever seen wave like flags from the line.

~

Friday after mowing the Pruitts' yard, I ask Miss Myrtie Mae, "How does someone go about being baptized?"

We're sitting in the gazebo, eating a salad filled with cherries, mandarin oranges, and marshmallows. She also made tiny crustless sandwiches spread with a dab of deviled ham. I'm famished, and it's all I can do to keep from wolfing down the whole meal in one bite.

Miss Myrtie Mae sets her fork down on her china plate, wipes a pink cloth napkin across her mouth, and says, "Why do you ask, Tobias?"

It's funny how a person can go from Toby to Tobias when they are asked certain questions. "No reason, really."

She looks at me, eyebrows hiked, and I realize she thinks I'm talking about *me*. So I tell her, "Oh, not me. A friend."

"I see." Her lips purse, and her voice drops to a deeper serious tone. "Well, one must consider this matter very seriously. It's not something you, I mean, your *friend*, should take lightly. The good Lord knows what state our mind is in when we make such a commitment. But it's a wonderful commitment, Tobias. The Christian life is not an easy life, but it brings such joy. And of course there is the gift of eternal life."

"But how does someone go about *getting* baptized?"

Her face pinches up. "You mean the procedure? First, you should talk to the preacher. I mean, your friend should talk to the preacher."

I try to picture Zachary walking through town to the church. Impossible. "What if he can't go see him? Does Reverend Newton make house calls?"

"I'm sure that can be arranged. Yes, I'm sure that would be no problem whatsoever for Reverend Newton." Miss Myrtie Mae loads the dishes onto the tray, humming "Just As I Am."

Today I dig up Miss Myrtie Mae's irises and separate the bulbs because she says they're too crowded to bloom. I also clear away the dried-up honeysuckle vine, whose sweet scent still lingers. So far, I've been lucky. No sign of the Judge anywhere. I wanted to ask Miss Myrtie Mae where he was, but I was afraid she'd call him outside.

Mowing east to west, I watch bees make lazy trails from flower to flower in the beds. I like mowing because it gives me time to think and plan. Not so much about Zachary, but about Scarlett. One thing I haven't tried yet is giving her a special gift. Heck, Dad won Mom over with a jelly jar of sunflowers. But what would Scarlett want? I don't have enough money to fix her gap. As I gather up the bags of grass clippings, I think about what to give her. I try to remember her room for ideas. She probably has every Bobby Sherman album. Maybe another bottle of Wind Song. Or another stuffed Autograph Hound. This time I'd write something really cool on it.

On the way to the garbage Dumpster, something hard hits my back. I swing around, dropping the bag. The Judge squats under the apple tree, plucking apples from a low branch and throwing them at me. *Pitching* them at me. "Think you can out-bat old Speedy, do ya, T.J.? Well, we didn't win first place last year for nothing."

I try to pick up the apples from a safe distance, but the old guy is pretty good. I'm amazed at how far the Judge can throw. He must have really been something on the pitcher's mound. Again and again he throws apples at me and I dodge them while trying to pick them up. We keep this going until Miss Myrtie Mae comes into the yard. When he sees her, the Judge hides an apple behind his back like a little kid caught stealing a cookie.

"Yoo-hoo!" she calls. "Here you are, Brother. Your *Life* magazine arrived."

Before I leave, Miss Myrtie Mae hands me a piece of paper. "Here, this is for your friend."

I look down at the paper. *John 3:16: For God so loved the world, that he gave his only begotten Son, that whosoever believeth in him should not perish, but have everlasting life."*

~

At home I check the mailbox before going inside. Among the bills is another letter from Mom. My chest tightens. This letter has a new address. I throw it on the dresser, on top of the other unopened one I received a few days ago.

Trying to find something for Scarlett, I wander inside my parents' room. Mom's perfume still lingers, and I almost expect her to prance out of her bathroom, saying, "Hey, Critter!" As always, her old guitar leans against the wall by her end table. Almost every night she sat on the bed in her pajamas, barefooted, strumming the guitar. She'd look at the ceiling as if words floated around up there, waiting to be plucked. Then she'd stop and scribble them in a notebook. I wonder why she didn't take the guitar with her if she knew she wasn't coming back.

I open the jewelry box on her dresser. The pearls are there, wrapped in a tissue. They feel cool to the touch, and I try to picture them on Scarlett. She'd probably wear them to school next year with her fuzzy blue sweater. I'd sit in back of her in class and watch her twirl the strand around her finger. Other girls would want to borrow them, but she wouldn't let them because *I* gave them to her.

After finding a box and wrapping the pearls with leftover Christmas paper, I sign my name on a card and head over to Scarlett's. Crossing the town square, I imagine her opening the gift and being speechless because she's never received anything as nice from Juan. She'll look at me with those baby blues and wonder why she overlooked my obvious good qualities.

But no one is home at Scarlett's house. Time is running out, and if I don't act quick, Scarlett will be back together with Juan. Before heading home, I leave the gift between the front and screen doors.

The minute I set foot in our house, I see Mom's velvet painting of Hank Williams hanging over the sofa and the framed form letter from Tammy Wynette. Guilt fills up in me from head to toe.

It was a stupid idea. Maybe if I race over to Scarlett's on my bike right now, I might be able to get the necklace before she returns. But on the way out the front door, I bump into Dad and Reverend Newton. A Bible is tucked under his arm.

"Toby," Reverend Newton says, "I understand we need to have a little talk."

Chapter Fifteen

Dad invites Reverend Newton into the living room. They start down the hall, but my feet stay glued to the floor. "Tobias," Dad says, glancing back. "You have company."

I shuffle to the living room, wondering how long Miss Myrtie Mae waited before calling the preacher. She probably picked up the phone as soon as I stepped off her porch.

Reverend Newton settles into Mom's plump chair, plopping the Bible onto his lap. I choose the straight chair on the far side of the room.

Dad remains standing. "Reverend Newton, would you like a cup of coffee?"

The reverend pushes at his bifocals. His heavy cheeks sag down to his jowls, giving him a bulldog look. "Is it already made?"

"No, but I'll be happy to make a fresh pot."

"Well, if it would be no trouble?"

"No trouble at all." Dad starts out, and Reverend Newton adds, "Two spoons of sugar and a tiny bit of milk." He holds up his fingers to show the amount.

"How about some cookies to go along with it?" Dad asks.

Reverend Newton rubs his round stomach. "Oooh, temptation. But I haven't eaten much all day. I might take one or two. If it's no trouble?"

"No trouble," Dad repeats, walking toward the kitchen. He looks relieved to have a reason to go.

I should warn the reverend that Dad's cookies aren't the sugar kind. In fact, he doesn't use sugar at all. They're bland as soda crackers, and once you take a bite, you're chewing for eternity.

Reverend Newton leans back. His elbows rest on the arms of the chair, and his chubby fingers lock together, forming a bridge. He studies me, and I study my shoes. "Toby, Toby, Toby. I must confess, I'm not here on a howdy-do visit. I'm here on a mission from the Lord." He sighs and his fingers tap his knuckles. "Is there anything you want to tell me, son?"

I shake my head. "No, sir."

He smiles. "Well, maybe I can make this a bit easier for you. I heard from the grapevine that you've been asking questions about the baptism. Am I correct?"

"Yes, sir, but—"

Reverend Newton holds up a hand, stopping my words. "No need to be ashamed. Every Christian goes through this time of turmoil." He leans forward. "The Lord is knocking on your heart, Toby. And, son, you better answer him."

"But—"

He raises his palm again. "It might help if I tell you about my own testimony. You see, I wasn't always walking the walk."

"You weren't?"

"No, no, indeed. I was a tax collector for the IRS. Looking back now, I kind of fancied myself as a modern day Zacchaeus. I enjoyed the misery I placed on others. I loved that power. I was *greedy* for power." He shivers like he is trying to shake off his past and continues rattling on and on.

I sink low into the chair. Reverend Newton is giving me my own personal sermon. I'm relieved when Dad appears with a mug of coffee and a plate of his cookies.

Reverend Newton takes a sip, closes his eyes, and smiles. "Ahh! Good coffee, Otto. By the way, heard from Opalina?"

Dad picks up the plate. "Have a cookie."

"Don't mind if I do." He leans forward, peers over his bifocals, and examines every cookie before he selects the biggest one. "Heard about that fire. It's a shame. Grand Ole Opry and all. Will they build a new one?" He waves the cookie with each word like a band conductor waving his baton.

I feel my body heating up.

"Fire?" Dad asks.

"Yes, what a shame. We must add the good folks of Nashville to our prayer list. And we sure do miss Opalina's solos. That voice is a gift from God."

Dad studies me and I squirm, wishing I could vanish.

"Getting back to your baptism. Your mother is going to be proud of you, Toby." Reverend Newton takes a bite of the cookie and frowns. He chews and chews and chews. Finally he swallows and chases it down with a swig of coffee. He winks at Dad. "These aren't Opalina's, are they, Otto? Good thing the Lord put women on this earth." He sets down the cookie and turns his focus to me. I feel his eyes reach into mine. He is digging. Digging for my soul. "Would you like to come down this week when I give the altar call?"

I can't stand it anymore. "Reverend Newton, my friend wants to be baptized. Not me."

Reverend Newton is quiet. He looks at me a long minute, then turns to Dad, who's leaning back in the recliner, feet up, hands clasped behind his neck.

"Who is your friend, son?"

"I can't tell you. I mean—he doesn't even know I'm talking about him."

Reverend Newton looks like I told him someone drove over his dog. Disappointed, he says, "Well, tell your friend I'm willing to listen."

"I will."

"And I will be honored to baptize him."

"I'll tell him."

The reverend stands.

"Oh, Reverend Newton?"

He smiles, hopeful. "Yes?"

"What would my friend need to do to be baptized?"

He frowns and after a long pause says, "First he should respond to our altar call. He can wait till the fourth stanza if he wants. He must confess he's a sinner. Then we'll schedule him in our baptistery. He'd be the tenth person to be baptized in our brand-new baptistery." Reverend Newton says that as if Zachary would win a big prize. Kind of like the time the IGA grocery store gave Earline a color TV for being the ten-thousandth customer.

Reverend Newton walks toward the door. "Otto,

thank you for the coffee and the cookies." Before leaving, he turns and shakes his finger at me. "Toby, if the Lord is knocking, you better let him on in. Otto, hope to see you in church Sunday."

"Good-bye, Reverend," Dad says.

The door closes and Dad stands before me, his arms crossed over his chest. I wonder what will be first—the baptism or the fire. "Toby, what is this about a fire at the Grand Ole Opry?"

I shrug, doing my best to sound innocent. "I have no idea. Somebody must have misunderstood me. Look how the baptism thing got all mixed up."

"Speaking of which—I hope that you haven't overstepped your boundaries as a friend. Someone's spiritual life is their own doings." He picks up the plate of cookies. "The reverend left before I could send him home with the rest of these. It would have been no trouble. No trouble at all." He winks at me and takes the plate into the kitchen.

I can't believe Dad let me off so easy. Maybe he really believes me about the fire being gossip. But I don't have time to figure out why. I've got to get the pearls back. With any luck, I'll arrive at Scarlett's house before she returns and finds them.

I race over on my bike and park outside the fence. But it's too late. Mrs. Stalling's car is parked in the driveway. I wonder if they went inside through the garage and didn't notice the package.

Through their front window, I see Mrs. Stalling at the stove and Scarlett setting the table. The TV is on, and Tara sits in front of it wearing Mickey Mouse ears. Quietly I walk up the steps to the porch and open the screen door. The package is gone. I walk back down to the sidewalk and glance again through the window, trying to see if Scarlett is wearing them. She's not. Tara stands and jumps like a kangaroo over to the table. *Hop, hop, hop.* Shiny pearls flop against her chest.

That little brat. That little, sticky finger brat. There's got to be a way to get the pearls back. I could wait for her to come outside in the morning and when she least expects it—

A horn sounds from the street and I jump. Kate is behind the wheel, and Cal is in the back of the pickup, waving his arm. "Come on! The ladybugs are here!"

For a second, the pearls vanish from my mind. I follow the truck on my bike to the train depot, where Kate signs a paper for the ladybugs. Then the three of us load the crates into the truck. Each crate holds two sacks filled with ladybugs. There must be millions of them. They'll make a great sight tonight at the Ladybug Waltz.

Seeing those crates stacked in the bed of the truck makes me think of Wayne. I look at Cal. He's all grins. My stomach knots up because I'm thinking about that letter and wondering what Cal is going to do when Wayne writes back. He's bound to mention it.

While we load the crates, Cal asks, "What did you find out about the baptism?"

I want to tell him the baptism has ruined my life. I'd have Mom's pearls in my hands right this minute if Reverend Newton hadn't visited me. Instead I tell him what the reverend said Zachary would need to do.

"Think he'll do it?" I ask.

"Sure," Cal says, always the optimist.

Enough is going on in my life to give me ulcers, but right now I put everything aside because this moment only comes once a year. I race the truck back home and win. After all, Kate is driving. In their front yard, Mrs. McKnight is trimming her roses. "Ladybugs arrive?"

"Yes, ma'am!" we holler together.

"Cal," she says, "you and Kate get washed up. Dinner is almost ready. And, Kate, sweetheart, set the table."

"See you in an hour," Cal says as he runs into the house, Kate following him.

I start to turn around, but Mrs. McKnight says, "Toby?"

"Yes, ma'am?"

"I was thinking about your mom today."

My stomach burns.

"I know you must miss her. Goodness, I miss her. She always seemed to have a song in her head and a smile on her face."

I tuck my hands in my pockets and dig my heel into the grass.

"It takes a brave woman to go after her dreams these days. You should be proud of her." She wipes her forehead with the back of her hand, moving a few dark curls away from her face. "Sometimes people don't feel complete until they go after their dreams. Even I have a few dreams of my own."

"You do?" I say, wishing I hadn't sounded surprised.

She laughs. "I know I don't look like I would, but I do. It's nothing glamorous like your mom's. I've always wanted to travel around the southeastern part of the country, searching for old roses."

"Oh," I say, nodding like I understand the greatness of it. But of course I don't.

She bends down and smells one of her perfect blooms. "I'd love to tromp through old graveyards and around neighborhoods where some of those roses grow. It would be exciting to discover a lost rose breed." She trims a faded bloom off the bush.

Just then a dark blue Chevrolet pulls up in front of the McKnight home and I'm grateful that Mrs. McKnight's company will allow me to escape this conversation. But as I'm about to dash off, two men in army officer uniforms step out.

Mrs. McKnight glances their way, and her face pales. She returns to cutting the blooms. "That would be nice," she says, her voice small and quivering.

I look at the McKnight house. Kate passes by the window, carrying a stack of plates, and I wonder if I should go get her. But my stomach is queasy, and my knees feel weak.

The men step into the yard and walk toward us. Mrs. McKnight keeps trimming the roses, only now she is trimming the new blooms too. She is chopping away the blooms and the stems. And with each step the men take toward her, the bush gets smaller. Her hands shake and her breathing becomes heavy and she ignores the men who are now in front of us. "Mrs. McKnight?" one man says.

She shakes her head and cuts, cuts, cuts, cuts. Thorns tear tiny scratches in her hands as the stems fall to the ground. Kate is staring out the window now, and I'm silently pleading for her to come and stand where I am standing.

"Mrs. McKnight," the man says, "is your husband at home? You might want to have him with you."

"No," she says, not looking, just cutting away the bush. It is now so short she is bending over to reach it. "No!" she cries, falling to her knees. "Not my Wayne! Not my boy!" She drops the clippers and her hands cover her face, muffling her cries as she rocks.

Both men exchange concerned looks. One officer steps toward her, then squats beside her. "We're sorry, ma'am. We truly are."

Kate is outside, hurrying toward her mom, and I know that I have willed her here. Because I don't know what to do. And, God, I want to know what to do. But all I can think of is to run home, close my bedroom door, and shut out the rest of the world.

Chapter Sixteen

The day after the news comes, I get up at dawn and look out my window. Outside, Mr. McKnight is pulling their flag up the pole. With each yank of the rope, the flag climbs until it reaches the top. Then he lets it drop to half-mast. When he turns, I catch a glimpse of his face. His lips press tightly together and his thick eyebrows touch, forming a *V* in the middle of his forehead. Soon after, Dad, who has been drinking coffee on the porch, digs our flag out of the closet. By the time eight rolls around, every flag on Ivy Street hangs from its flagpole.

The ladybugs stay sealed in their crates, stacked in the McKnights' backyard. I worry that without water they'll die. But later Cal goes out back and walks over to the garden hose on the side of the house. I hold the shade away from the window and watch him. He slowly unravels the hose until it stretches the length of the yard, then drags it over to the crates. After turning the water on full blast, he aims the nozzle straight up. Not one drop hits the ladybugs. A few moments later he throws down the hose and heads to the stack of crates. I hold my breath, hoping he'll spray the ladybugs. But he leaves the hose on the ground and the water runs onto the grass, disappearing. Then he kicks one of the crates, causing it to thump to the ground. He kicks it over and over again like a soccer ball. It's the first time I've ever seen him angry. He didn't even get mad when Kate punched him in the mouth. A moment later he returns the crate to the stack, turns off the hose, and goes back inside.

It's the day before the funeral. I haven't left my house in three days. Like Zachary, I watch the world from my window. Billy and Mr. McKnight leave for the cotton fields each morning, but Cal and Kate stay home with their mom. I haven't seen Mrs. McKnight since that day the men came. The wind has stripped away most of the petals on her roses, and the few blooms that remain are faded.

It seems like our town has closed down these days leading up to the funeral. Old people still sit on their porches and talk, but their conversations aren't sprinkled with laughter anymore. Since the news, little kids haven't played outside, as if their moms are afraid someone might snatch them out of their yards and send them off to war.

Every day the phone rings on and off, but I don't answer it. This morning it rings fifteen times. I'm afraid it's Cal, and I don't know what to say to him. What do you say when your best friend's brother dies? And what if Cal has found out about the letter I wrote Wayne?

When the phone rings again, I yell out to no one, "Leave me alone!" and escape with a sack of food for Zachary. I place it on the trailer steps, knock, and hurry back home.

At supper Dad says, "Your mother called a few minutes ago. She tried to reach you this week, but you didn't answer."

I don't say anything. I just concentrate on spreading the butter over my roll. But I'm relieved to know that it wasn't Cal calling.

"She's concerned about you," Dad says. "She knows about Wayne."

I look up.

"Have you seen Cal?" he asks.

"No."

Dad's temples pulse and he stares at me like he doesn't know me. Finally he looks down at his plate, shakes his head, and takes a bite of turnips.

After dinner he watches the news, and when it shows a war scene, he clicks off the TV. Then he puts on a Mozart album and reads *Field & Stream*.

At seven Dad is ready to go to the wake. He stands in front of me, dressed in a white shirt, black pants, and a striped tie older than dirt. "Aren't you going?" he asks.

I shake my head again.

Dad snaps his tongue against the roof of his mouth. "He was Cal's brother."

"I know that."

He starts toward the door, jiggling the keys in his hand. "Toby, do we need to talk about something?"

"I just don't feel like going."

His hand rests on the doorknob. "Sometimes we have to do things we don't feel like doing." And with that, he leaves.

Sitting in my dark room, I shuffle Mom's unopened letters like a deck of cards and listen to Dad's door close and the truck drive off. For the next few minutes I hear car doors shutting and engines starting up and down the street. They're all going to the same place.

The place I can't bear to go. I want to remember Wayne hitting baseballs at a Buck's game, eating a Bahama Mama snow cone in front of Wylie Womack's stand, releasing the ladybugs in the middle of the cotton fields.

The ladybugs. I rush downstairs and out of the house, then sneak into the McKnights' backyard. I unwind the hose, screw on the spray nozzle, and adjust the water for a gentle flow. In the dark, with only the light from a cloud-filtered moon shining down on me, I wet down the ladybugs, thinking of Wayne and last year's Ladybug Waltz.

Last summer, the ladybugs arrived in early July. That night Wayne and the others stood out in the fields with sacks above their heads, releasing the ladybugs. The waltz was Wayne's idea. When he found out Dad liked classical music, Wayne asked him to pick out a song to play while the bugs took flight. Finding a new song for the past three years has become a tradition, but now when I think about it, I think it was Wayne's way of getting Dad involved because he knew Dad was shy.

I had always imagined going with Cal's family to the airport to pick Wayne up when his tour ended. I imagined him walking off the plane, dressed in his uniform, hugging his mom and Kate, shaking all the guys' hands, including mine. I guess I even imagined him taking me aside later and asking, "It was you that wrote that letter, wasn't it, buddy?" It would be our secret, kind of like a secret between brothers. Only now it would never be.

One foot into the house, I hear the phone ring, and without thinking I pick it up.

"Hello?"

"Toby?" Mom's voice comes in as clear as if she were calling from across the street. "Oh, thank goodness, Toby. I had a feeling you might be there. Are you okay?"

She doesn't let me answer. "You're like me. You can't handle sad. Give us mad, give us happy, but don't tear our hearts out. Oh, Critter, it's so good to hear you. . . . You there?"

"I'm here."

"Your dad, now, he's good at the sad things. But I always thought your dad teetered on being sad most days anyway. Some people are like that." Nothing has changed. She still rattles on and on.

"Critter, I'm thinking of you, honey. I know this is hard for you. I don't know what I would do if I lost you. They might as well dig another grave for me."

I know she's expecting me to say something, but I just stretch the phone cord across the room.

I recognize the tiny thumps, and I can almost see her tapping her long fingernails on a table. "I want you to come see me while there's still some summer left. Okay?"

I don't say a word.

"You can ignore me all you want, Toby, but I know you want to see me almost as much as I want to see you. I know you do. A mother knows this about her kid."

I count the soldiers on my dresser.

"I'm trying really hard here, Tob. Can't you see that?"

"I've got to go," I say quickly.

"I love y—"

I press down on the receiver and listen to the click cut off her words.

The morning of Wayne's funeral, I put on my sixth-grade graduation suit and tie. The sleeves are too short, and the jacket fits tight across my back. I check myself in the mirror, and right now I'm not thinking about Wayne or Cal or anybody else except Scarlett and hoping she doesn't see me in this monkey suit.

Dad stands in my doorway. "You ready?"

"I'll be there in a minute. Go ahead without me."

He pauses. "Cal will need you, Toby." His words are slow and deliberate, and I know he wants to add, *You better be there,* but he turns and leaves.

As soon as I hear the front door shut, I walk to my dresser. Over two hundred soldiers stand ready for battle. I knock one over, then another and then another. One at a time. Until no soldiers are standing.

A minute later I look out from our front porch. The sky is gray and lightning strikes through the clouds. A hearse from Landry's Funeral Home is parked outside the McKnights'. The walk to the church should only take a few minutes, but I drag out my bike from the garage and hop on. And instead of turning right, toward the church, I turn left, lean into the wind, and ride. I jump sidewalk curbs and skim corners on the turns. My bike and I become one, and we don't stop until we are in front of the Bowl-a-Rama.

A sign posted on the door reads, Closed Due to Funeral. I stare at my reflection in the glass and watch Wylie Womack's golf cart pull up behind me. "Hey, Wylie," I say, turning to face him.

Wylie's hair is smoothed back neatly in a ponytail, and he wears a wrinkled suit with a daisy tucked in the buttonhole. He holds out his hand, offering the space next to him.

I shake my head. "No, thanks, Wylie. I'm heading that way in a minute."

With a nod, Wylie takes off in the direction of the church, his folded wheelchair tucked in the back of the cart. Another streak of lightning branches across the sky, followed by thunder.

I start to knock on the Bowl-a-Rama's door, then notice it's already ajar. Inside the dark bowling alley, I call out, "Ferris." No one answers. Suddenly it dawns on me a thief could be walking around, taking advantage of an all-town-attended funeral. If he is, I don't want to be here.

As I'm about to leave, I hear someone clearing his throat in the cafe. A few steps closer, I discover Ferris sitting at a table in front of the window with the blinds closed, his head bent like he is praying over a bottle of Jim Beam.

"Ferris?" I move toward him. "You okay?"

He looks up. His eyes are red and puffy, and a clip-on tie hangs from one corner of the collar of his unbuttoned shirt. "Hey, Toby? Shouldn't you be at the funeral?"

"I'll get there. What's wrong?"

He digs out a handkerchief from his pocket and blows his nose, sounding like a foghorn. "Got a nasty cold," he says. He pours himself another drink. "Don't ever start drinking, Toby. Next to money, it's the root of all evil."

"Aren't you going to the funeral?"

Ferris shakes his head. "I'll pay my respects later. The McKnights will understand. They're good people." He looks up at me through his puffy eyes. "You better get a move on, boy. You'll be late."

I turn to leave and Ferris says, "You know what they say is true."

"What who says?"

"What everyone in town says about me going yellow. That's me, all right."

At first I don't know what the heck he's talking about, but then I figure he's referring to what happened to his leg and not serving in the Korean War. Maybe Wayne's death made Ferris remember. And I guess the Jim Beam helps him forget.

I creep backward out of the cafe and out of the Bowl-a-Rama, across the street to Zachary's trailer.

Zachary is looking out the window, his forehead pressed against the new glass. When I knock, he hollers, "Come in."

A foul odor nearly knocks me over as I enter. It smells rotten like a sewer. "What stinks?"

Zachary's face turns red. He's sitting in his love seat, looking at a *National Geographic* magazine. "This town stinks."

The smell is coming from inside the trailer, but I don't feel like arguing. "Don't you lock your door?"

"I kind of got out of the habit. Have a seat."

"You ought to lock your doors. Crooks live in small towns too." I yank off my suit coat, loosen my tie, and flop on the floor.

"Who died?" Zachary asks.

"How do you know someone died?"

"Well, for one thing, you're wearing a monkey suit. And the whole town's been quiet for the last four days. I've had only two knocks on the door. You and Kate. Neither one of you bothered to stay."

I've been in such a fog the last few days, I forgot about the sheriff's plans for Zachary. He should have been long gone by now. Maybe Wayne's death postponed them.

Zachary waits for me to answer. "Well? Who died?"

I try to sound casual. "A guy who was in Vietnam. He w-was—" I swallow. "He was really great." My eyes sting, and I bite down on my tongue.

Zachary notices. He turns his head and studies the wall. Outside, the thunder rolls again. "It's weird here," he says. "You get lightning and thunder, but no rain."

"We get rain. Well, sometimes."

"Yeah," Zachary says, "that war is bad stuff."

I nod, swallowing the big lump in my throat. I want to change the subject. Right now I'd even listen to his lies about going to Europe. I don't know what to say, so I blurt out, "If you talk to the minister, he'll baptize you."

Zachary stares a hole in me. "I'm not getting baptized."

"What's the big deal?"

"Why are you so interested in my soul? I never took you as the religious type."

I glance up at the bookshelf and see the albums. "Where else have you been?"

He smiles, and I'm relieved I've picked something that he'll talk about for a while so my mind might escape thoughts of Wayne's funeral. I can hardly smell the stink anymore. "Holland," he says. "Have I told you about Holland?"

"No." I lean my head against the wall and pretend to listen to him talk about Dutch windmills and tulips, but it's no use. I can't stop thinking about Cal and his family. And Wayne.

Zachary sounds like the book reports we give in geography—naming capitals, agriculture products, and rivers. He has passed Holland and moved on to Switzerland when we hear the bugle. He stops talking while taps plays far off in the cemetery. A shiver runs through my body.

When it's finished, Zachary says, "Wow! I've only heard that on TV."

Later, someone knocks at the trailer door.

"It's open!" Zachary hollers, and I realize when he says that, he's grown sort of comfortable in Antler.

The door opens and Cal walks in, hands in his pants pockets and tie loose around his neck. A sheen of sweat covers his face, which is redder than his hair. He stares at me like I've betrayed him. My chest tightens because I know that's exactly what I've done.

"Pull up a seat," Zachary says, holding his hand out to the floor. "I was telling Cowboy about Switzerland."

Cal's hands pop out of his pockets, and dollar bills are crammed in his fists. "Here."

He throws the money at me. Coins clank to the floor and join the one-dollar and five-dollar bills. "Here's your forty-six bucks I owe you. Now we're even."

I don't move one inch.

Zachary seems flustered, looking from me to Cal. "What's going on?"

"You both deserve each other!" Cal yells. His eyes flicker, and tears make rivers down his cheeks. "You're both big fat liars!"

He turns toward Zachary. "Switzerland? You've never been there. You've never been anywhere besides county fairs and one-ring circuses. You're in a freak show. You *are* a freak." He marches over to the curtain and yanks it back. The smell is stronger. "See."

Behind the curtain is a toilet—a regular-size toilet with handles attached to the floor to help Zachary pull himself up. A shower stall is in the corner, with no door. A mop with a washcloth tied to it leans next to the shower wall. And between the stall and toilet are books. Lots and lots of books with titles like *Switzerland* and *A Pictorial Guide to Holland* and *Seattle Sights*.

Zachary studies the floor, reminding me of that night in the back of the truck at the drive-in. He is trying to disappear.

Cal turns toward me. "And you—everybody knows you're lying about your mom. She's not coming back. She's never, ever coming back. Like Wayne!"

He heads toward the door, turns, and yells, "IT STINKS IN HERE!" Then he storms out of the trailer. But I don't follow. I sit there on the floor with forty-six dollars at my feet while my gut tears into a million pieces and sheets of rain pour from the sky.

Chapter Seventeen

The day after Wayne's funeral, Dad barely speaks to me. And although he's usually quiet, this quiet is different. It's heavy and thick, and I feel like I'm drowning in it. After breakfast I head outside, looking for a place to escape. But there's nowhere in Antler to escape. Everyone in town except Ferris and me went to the funeral, and they probably all know that we didn't. I head over to the Bowl-a-Rama.

The sky is clear again. Except for a few mud puddles, everything looks fresh and clean from the rain. But it's also humid and sticky. Across the street at Zachary's trailer, I see Sheriff Levi's car and Coy Davis's pickup. Coy pumps the septic tanks for the folks who live in the country around Antler, and right now his wide hose is attached to the bottom of the trailer.

Inside the Bowl-a-Rama, Ferris leans over the soda

fountain counter in the cafe, rubbing his temples and groaning. "Of all days for Ima Jean to call in sick. Don't ever start drinking, Toby. Next to money—"

"It's the root of all evil."

Ferris flinches. "Who told you that?"

"Oh, I've heard it once or twice." He must have forgotten our entire conversation yesterday.

"I'm going to have to close today. I can't cook and clean and wait on tables at the same time."

"I'll help you, Ferris."

He studies me a moment, then nods. "You got a job. The pay ain't great, but the food ain't too shabby."

The Good Luck, Opalina! sign is gone, and I figure Cal is right. Everyone in town knows Mom isn't coming back. Cal knew all along. But he never said a word, just like he never let on that he knew Zachary had never visited all those places he had claimed.

While Ferris cooks today's special—barbecue beef and potato salad—I put napkins and silverware on the tables.

"What side does the fork go on?" I ask him.

"It don't matter. Just so you put it in grabbin' distance. I ain't had a customer complain about my table etiquette yet."

An hour before the main lunch crowd hits, I set out the ketchup bottles and the salt and pepper shakers.

Sheriff Levi comes in, sits at the counter, and orders a glass of iced tea and a hamburger. Ferris slaps a frozen patty on the grill and talks to the sheriff through the kitchen window that looks out onto the counter. "What's all that carrying on over at the trailer?"

"Mercy, Ferris! His holding tank needed emptying. Couldn't you smell it?"

"Nope," Ferris says. "I've never been much good at smelling anything. That's why I wasn't worth a dad-blame thing at hunting. My daddy said the best hunters can smell their prey. Any word on that fella coming back for Zachary?"

I take my time arranging the salt and pepper shakers, making my way closer to the counter.

"Nope," the sheriff says, "not a word. I put off dealing with that for far too long. This morning I had to make a call to social services."

"That's a shame," Ferris says. "Jalapeños?"

"You betcha. Not too many, though. They tear up my insides." I pour more tea in the sheriff's glass, hoping he'll keep talking about Zachary. "Did some research on the boy," he says. "His only relative is an uncle, and he's in jail serving time for armed robbery."

Ferris places the buns on the grill. "What happened to his parents?"

"Couldn't find out a thing about the father except

that he left when Zachary was a baby. But his mother died two years ago—Iola Beaver. Found her in the *New York Times* obituaries. That's how I found the name of her minister, too. I called him up. He told me her funeral drew quite a crowd. It was a circus. Media showed up. She was like her son—huge. They even had to make a special casket to fit her. The minister said, when everybody saw Zachary at the funeral, things got way out of hand—people pushing and shoving for a better view, cameras and microphones aimed at Zachary."

Ferris snaps his tongue. "People don't know when to quit."

I think of the picture of the man in the *Guinness Book of World Records* who was buried in a piano case. Now it all makes sense. Zachary probably didn't get baptized because he didn't want a crowd gathering like at his mother's funeral. It's weird how Zachary didn't mind people traipsing through the trailer, staring at him, but being outside in the real world was different.

Ferris pours some potato chips on the plate next to the hamburger, then sets the plate in front of Sheriff Levi. "What about this Paulie Rankin guy? Is he on the up-and-up?"

"Believe it or not," says Sheriff Levi, "he's the legal

guardian. Before Zachary's uncle went to jail, he signed over guardianship to Paulie Rankin. I just wish I knew where the heck he is now." He takes a big bite of the burger, and a few jalapeño slices slip out.

"When are they coming to get the boy?"

"Saturday," the sheriff says with a mouth full of hamburger. He swallows, then washes it down with tea. "I told the social worker I'd keep an eye on him until then. She needs the time to find out where to put him. He's a special case. Not anyone will take in a six-hundred-pound teenager."

"Yes, sir," Ferris says. "That boy could eat you out of house and home." He and the sheriff smirk, but the smiles fall from their faces as quickly as they came. Clearing his throat, Ferris walks over to the register and pushes a key. The cash drawer opens with a *ding*. He flips up one of the hinges, pulls out an envelope, and hands it to the sheriff. "Here's that money Rankin sent. Give it to the boy so he has a little something."

Sheriff Levi nods and tucks the envelope in his shirt pocket.

A million solutions tumble together in my head. Why can't Zachary live with Ferris? Or the sheriff? Or Miss Myrtie Mae? But Ferris lives in a small room in the Bowl-a-Rama. The sheriff seems to prefer living with dogs, and Miss Myrtie Mae has her hands full with the crazy old judge. I'm wishing more and more that any second Paulie Rankin would return to town and whisk Zachary away to his life on the road. That would be better than living with strangers.

The usual lunch crowd starts trickling in—the Shriners and farmers, Miss Myrtie Mae and the Judge, and Earline. I quickly learn this was the worst place to hide. They all talk about the funeral.

"It was beautiful and sad," Earline says, rubbing the side of her nose. Today she's without her blazer, and her short-sleeved dress shows the fatty backs of her upper arms. And though Earline doesn't say, I know she knows that I wasn't there because she mentions Cal several times—how brave he was, not even crying when his entire family did, how he shook everyone's hand and thanked them for coming to the funeral, how he handed Kate his handkerchief. I feel like the biggest jerk in Texas.

When the lunch crowd dies down, I fill the sink with sudsy hot water. A second later Ferris says, "Toby, someone is here to see you."

Scarlett stands in the doorway wearing a pink sun-dress and Dr. Scholl's wooden sandals. Her toenails match her dress. I'm wishing I had on anything but an undershirt and the huge white apron tied around my waist.

Ferris watches us from the stove, a silly grin on his whiskered face. When he sees me frowning, he clears his throat and turns back around.

Scarlett steps toward me, holding out a box—the box I used for the pearls. "Toby, thanks for the necklace, but I can't keep it."

All the worrying and plotting I did, wondering how to get those pearls back, and she solves my problem so easy. But still, I'm disappointed. "Why?" I ask.

"It's too nice a gift, and my mom said I have to return it to you. And . . ." She blushes.

"And what?"

"Toby . . . I just don't like you that way."

Now I blush. I look at Ferris's back, but if he heard, he doesn't act like it. He keeps scrubbing the grill.

Scarlett glances over her shoulder at Ferris and lowers her voice. "I mean, I like you. I really like you. Just not *that* way."

She starts to leave.

I want to block the door, but my feet won't budge. "Scarlett?"

When she turns around, I try to imagine a wart on her perfect nose or a deep crooked scar mapping across her smooth cheek. But I can't. I feel helpless, desperate. "You can still keep the pearls. It could be a friendship gift."

"I wouldn't wear them."

"Why not?"

"Well . . . pearls kind of remind me of something an old lady would wear. I'm sorry."

I smile. "That's okay. My mom never wore them either."

Scarlett tucks a strand of hair behind her ear and tilts her head in a way that makes me melt. "Toby Wilson, you are the nicest boy in Antler." She walks out of the kitchen and out of the cafe, her sandals slapping the linoleum floor.

Ferris turns around, holding a sponge. "There goes one little heartbreaker. You okay, buddy?"

I can only nod.

Chapter Eighteen

Ima Jean is still sick, so I work another day for Ferris. After finishing the dishes and wiping down the counters, Ferris hands me a plate piled high with today's special—spaghetti and meatballs. "Take this over to Zachary on your way home."

I don't feel like seeing him, and I doubt he feels like seeing me much either. I leave the plate on the steps, dashing off after I knock on his door.

When I've almost reached home, I see Juan Garcia waiting on my front steps. He leans back, propped on his elbows, chewing a piece of Johnson grass. My breath quickens and my legs wobble with each step.

As I get closer, I notice a cardboard box next to him—the kind used for moving or maybe for burying short eighth graders that give other guys' girlfriends pearl necklaces. I stop a few yards away from him, wipe my clammy palms on my jeans, and say, "Hey."

Juan frowns and wrinkles his forehead. "Hey, man. How's it going?"

"Fine," I manage to say. I glance around, trying to plan an escape route. Juan is blocking my entrance to the front door.

"Too bad about Wayne," Juan says, standing and walking up to me.

"Yeah. He was a great guy." I look up at Juan.

"Nice house," he says.

"Thanks. It's old." I try to downplay our home because I know Juan lives on the Mexican side of town, where the shabbiest houses are.

"We even get mice sometimes," I add.

He nods, but I get the feeling he isn't thinking about my house. "I need to ask you something."

"What's that?"

"Scarlett . . . she says you're the nicest guy."

"Me? I got her fooled." My voice squeaks, and I hope it doesn't sound as scared as I'm feeling.

He frowns and I quickly say, "We're just friends." And the truth of those words sting.

"She says I should be more like you." He studies me, his jaw tilted and eyes narrowed.

"She does?"

"Yeah." Juan squares his shoulders. "What does *that* mean?"

"Heck, I don't know. I'm just nice to her." Then I remember what Scarlett told me at Gossimer Lake. "I mean, I guess I wouldn't stand her up or anything." As soon I say it, I regret it.

He grimaces. "Is that what this is all about, her grandpa's party?"

"I guess it was really important to her."

Juan looks away, his head bobbing. Big sweaty circles under his arms mark his T-shirt. He shakes his head. "Man!"

"She said you didn't even give her a reason." I hope I haven't said too much, but his eye stays focused on the street and his head keeps bobbing.

"I had something to do," he says. "I try to talk to her, but she hangs up when I call and when I go over there, she slams the door in my face."

"I know she likes you." I swallow.

"Yeah?"

"Believe me, I know."

Juan smiles, shaking his head. "Women!"

I shake my head too. "Yeah, women!"

"And how do you handle the little sister?"

"Tara?"

"Yeah, Scarlett says you're really nice to her."

"Can't help you there," I say.

Juan scowls. "Man, that kid's a brat." He lifts up the

box, and I notice a pants leg and a shirtsleeve hanging out of it. Right away I recognize them as Wayne's. The box must be filled with his clothes.

Juan notices me looking at Wayne's clothes and quickly stuffs them back into the box. For a second he looks embarrassed, but then he jerks back his head and walks out the gate.

Then it hits me that maybe the reason Juan didn't go to Scarlett's grandpa's fancy party wasn't because he had something to do, but because he had nothing to wear. I watch him walk away in his soiled T-shirt and flip-flops worn thin at the soles. And I don't know if it's because of his old clothes or because I feel lucky to have every bone in my body in one piece, but I take off and catch up to him. "Juan, can you be in front of your house in a half hour?"

"Sure. Why?"

"You'll see." I head back home, then turn around. Juan is already a few houses away. Cupping my hands around my mouth, I holler, "Hey, Juan, you might want to clean up real quick."

With Mom's green nylon scarf tied to my handlebar, I ride my bike down Scarlett's street. A few doors from her house, I pass Tara in a neighbor's driveway. She's holding hands with a little girl and the girl's mother.

They're new in town, and I guess they haven't gotten to know Tara the Terror yet. "We're going to the Dairy Queen," Tara tells me as she heads to the car with them.

"Have fun," I call from my bike. A new Dairy Queen has opened up in the next town over. It's a few miles away, and that means I won't have to worry about Tara tagging along behind us.

After parking on the sidewalk, I tuck the scarf in my pocket and find Scarlett playing solitaire on the steps of her front porch. "Hi."

Scarlett glances up and looks back down to the cards. "Hi." She turns over a seven of hearts and places it on top of the eight of clubs, then keeps playing like I'm not even there.

"I have a surprise for you."

"Toby," she says. "No more gifts, please."

Her words kill me, but I swallow and say, "You'll like this one. Trust me."

I pull out Mom's scarf. "I have to tie this around your eyes."

"Toby."

"Trust me."

She giggles as I tie on the scarf, trying not to smell her shampooed hair or perfume. Then I take small steps, guiding her to my bike. "Swing your leg over," I say, holding my bike steady.

She starts to raise her leg, then puts it down. "What are we doing?"

"Come on. You'll be safe. I promise."

She swings her leg over, and her ankle hits the pedal. "Ouch." It leaves a white scrape on her tanned skin.

"Sorry," I say, helping her onto the banana seat. "I should have tied on the scarf *after* you were on the bike." I slip in front of her. "Hang on."

She locks her arms around my waist, and I try to push back thoughts of our dance at Gossimer Lake. I launch with my feet, and after a wobbly start we're off, pedaling down the street and heading toward the highway.

Scarlett squeals and her grip tightens. It's hard to tell if she's petrified or loving the adventure. Once the coast is clear, I cross the highway and the railroad tracks.

"Oh, my gosh!" She giggles as we ride over the bumps. "Where are we going?"

"You'll see soon enough."

This is the moment I've dreamed of—riding through town on my bike with the girl of my dreams holding on to me for dear life. As we cross over the railroad tracks, Scarlett lets out three short shrieks. I have no idea which house is Juan's because Mom never let me ride through this neighborhood. But down the road, Juan is in his yard, swinging the golf club like a pro. He's wearing a red sports shirt I recognize immediately as Wayne's.

When Juan catches a glimpse of who is sitting behind me, he grins. As I get closer, I notice he's standing in a long strip of mowed weeds with a few golf balls scattered about. All along I guess Juan used the number-five iron to practice golf. I remember Juan's T-shirt with Super Mex scribbled across it and feel stupid that I didn't know what it meant before. That must be his big plan, to be like Lee Trevino—Super Mex.

I stop inches from Juan's feet, carefully step off the bike, and pull off Scarlett's blindfold. When she sees him, she smiles, then quickly frowns. "Toby, you shouldn't have done this. Take me back."

"You'll have to walk," I say. "I've got to get home."

"I'll walk you home," Juan says. "I've got to talk to you."

Scarlett doesn't move, and I'm thinking I've made a big mistake. Now Juan and Scarlett will be mad at me.

"Como sé llama?" Juan says.

Scarlett shyly smiles at Juan. "*Me llamo* Scarletta."

"*Muy bien,*" Juan says. "You remember."

Slowly Scarlett gets off the bike and steps toward him. My chest feels like it's squeezing my heart.

I turn my bike toward town, but before I can take off, Scarlett touches my shoulder, leans over, and kisses my cheek. She whispers, "I still think you're the nicest boy in Antler."

I start pedaling and I don't look back.

Chapter Nineteen

I'm drained and exhausted from playing Cupid. I don't want to do anything tonight but turn on the television and watch *The Flip Wilson Show*. Inside, Dad strings his fishing pole at the kitchen table. Another one lies next to it. "Toby," he says, "get your grubbies on. We're going fishing."

Lake Kiezer is quiet. All the water-skiers have quit for the day. Some campers load up and drive off. Except for a boat filled with old men fishing, Dad and I are the only ones on the water.

We sit across from each other in Dad's dinghy, which we've rowed to his favorite spot. Usually fishing makes me want to jump out of my skin from the stillness of it all, but today the quiet calms me.

I never liked fishing, and I've managed to avoid it for the last three years. The first time Dad took me, I must have been four or five years old. He always let me play with the worms in the shed while he worked. Back then, I had fun playing with their wiggly bodies and burying them in the dirt. The first day he took me fishing, I cried when he stuck one of my pals on a hook. He tried to show me how much fun it was to catch fish, then turn them loose, but I wasn't happy until we packed up and went home.

As I got older, it wasn't the worms on the hooks that bothered me as much as the boredom of it. There's too much waiting involved.

The sun sits low in the sky, and I figure we've got another full hour of daylight. Dad reels in a bass, and it's a looker. I can even imagine it cooked up on the skillet with a side order of Ferris's hush puppies.

"She's a beauty, isn't she?" Dad says, holding her up for me to see. "At least four pounds, I expect." He slips his finger in her mouth and frees her from the hook, then gently lowers her into the water.

"Why do you do that?" I ask, annoyed.

"Throw her back?"

I nod.

"She's done me a favor, now I'm doing her one."

"What favor did she do you?"

"Let me enjoy the thrill of catching her."

"Oh, yeah, that's thrilling, all right."

"Not exciting enough for you?"

I shrug.

He rebaits his hook, then casts out beautifully, his line gliding through the air and diving gracefully into the water. He reels in the line, taking up the slack. "Toby, I grew up with enough excitement to last two lifetimes. When he wasn't working, your grandfather constantly entertained clients and politicians. Our house swarmed with *important* people. His schedule was filled with things that had nothing to do with his family and everything to do with getting ahead. I would have killed to have had one moment like this with him."

I don't know what to say because my life seems to have been filled with moments like this with Dad and I've always felt they were too quiet, especially now with Mom gone. I reel in my line to check my bait. The worm is still there. I cast toward a big rock and watch the ripples smooth out on the water.

"Nice cast," Dad says. "Antler offered me something that Dallas never did. I can be myself here. Maybe it's dull to you. I'm sorry about that. I guess it was too dull for your mom."

"Why did you marry her?"

He frowns as if he's angry, but he looks toward the

horizon and his lips slide into a smile. "The first time I ever laid eyes on your mom, she was singing in a rodeo at Caprock Arena. That tiny little thing was filled with so much life." He keeps looking at the horizon, and it's as if he's not talking to me, but to himself. "Passionate about her dreams, even back then. I guess I thought like me, her dreams belonged to her youth and that she'd be happy with the simple life. But that was my dream. It wasn't right for me to expect her to change." He turns his head toward me. "So if there is any blaming to do, aim it my way."

When he says that, I realize that's exactly what I've wanted to do, but now I feel numb and I don't know who to blame. So after a long moment I say, "I don't blame you, Dad."

"Then don't blame her either. She loves you, Toby. You need to let her love you."

A lump gathers in my throat. "Do you think you'll get back together?"

"I can't answer that." His temples pulse and he looks out onto the water, where the sun glistens. "I can tell you this, though. You're a lucky person if you go through life and have one person need you. And you've got more than a couple that do."

I wonder if he's talking about Cal.

He looks straight at me. "I know Wayne meant a lot to you, Toby. But he was Cal's brother. Not yours."

His words sting, and I feel a rush of anger rising in me.

"Hear me out," Dad says. "I've let you slide on a few things lately. I know that your mom leaving has had a big effect on you. But you should have been at that funeral."

I nod because the lump crowds my throat and won't let me talk.

"Cal needs you."

"But I messed up. I can't go to the funeral now."

Something tugs at Dad's line, and his shoulders tense. The fish pulls the slack out of his line, and Dad slowly turns the handle on his reel. Then his shoulders relax in place. "Ah, he let go."

He pulls in his line to check the bait. The worm is missing. As he digs for another one, he says, "You asked me the other day if I ever wanted to be a lawyer. I did. Only to make my dad proud. But I messed up and failed the bar exam. Twice."

I don't know what to say, so I don't say anything. I've always thought Dad was kind of boring, but I never thought about him failing at anything.

Dad hooks the worm, then casts again. "You're right, Toby. It's too late for the funeral. But today is another tough day for Cal. Today his family is getting the rest of Wayne's stuff."

My head swims. "You mean like letters?"

"Yeah, letters, clothes, books, whatever he had. Cal will need you. Don't let him down now."

My line starts to bob, but all I can think about is my letter to Wayne and if Cal will ever forgive me.

~

One nice thing about fishing with Dad is there are no fish to clean after returning home. I smell fishy, though. I think about taking a shower before dinner, but when I look out the window over my dresser, I see Cal coasting his bike down the driveway.

I slam the drawer shut and rush outside to get my bike. I take off after him. He's already turned off Ivy Street, and I wonder if he's headed right or left. I choose right and pedal fast. I catch a glimpse of him on Elm Street and race toward him. He rides at a slow pace, but as I get closer, he glances back and speeds up. I pedal harder, trying to meet his pace, but he's faster than me and becomes a blue blur way down the road. I lean forward, working with the wind at my back. Finally I gain enough speed and we're just inches from each other. If I reach out, I could grab him.

Cal stands, breathing hard, pedaling like mad. Ignoring me, he focuses straight ahead on the road. He turns left. I turn left. He turns right, and so do I. I am his shadow. Then Cal turns sharply back to the left, but this time when I try to follow, I fall. The deep scrape on my knee throbs and blood pools to the surface. Instead of stopping and helping me as Cal would have a week ago, he presses on.

I study my knee and think about giving up. What use is it to follow? But I ignore the scrape, straighten my handlebar, then hop on my seat again. Cal heads west toward Gossimer Lake. I know he's going to the lake because that's the only thing worth aiming for out there. By taking the shortcut through the alley and crossing the road to the other end of the lake, I reach it the moment he does.

But when he sees me, he keeps pedaling and doesn't stop even when he reaches the water. He plunges in, bike and all, disappearing under the murky surface. I hop off my bike and run in, searching for him. He stands, his curls wet and clinging flat to his head like a bathing cap.

"Get outta here!" he yells, kicking water in my face.

And when I don't, he slugs me on the arm. I still don't move, and he punches me again. My arm throbs in pain. He starts to swing toward me and I step back and yell, "Are you crazy? Cut it out!"

"Where's my bike?" He squats and his arms hunt frantically through the water.

I join him in the search, and finally I feel a handlebar jabbing my stomach. "Here!"

Together we manage to drag the bike out of the mud and water. We flop down on the grass, soaked to the bone. "That hurt," I say, stroking my arm.

We look at each other and laugh. And it's not just a chuckle, but a great big belly laugh. It feels good to laugh together like old times—like before Wayne died. But as much as I'm enjoying the moment, I stop and say, "I have to tell you something—something I did."

Cal's face drops. "I already know."

"You know about the letter?"

He nods, looks away, and rakes his fingers through his damp hair. "It should have been me. I should have written him." He swallows, and I hear it slide down his throat.

"I . . . I should have gone to the funeral."

He picks up a rock and skips it across the water. "The army gave us a flag."

"Cool," I say, thinking that's the least they could do.

"Want to see it sometime?"

"Yeah, I'd like that."

And for a long time, we don't say another word. We

just listen to the cicadas and the crickets while the setting sun beams down on our soaked bodies. Then Cal grins, his black tooth showing. "Well, I guess you finally got baptized."

"Yeah," I say. "Now if only Zachary could."

We laugh, but then we stop dead cold and stare at each other, wide-eyed. And in this moment, I realize one reason it's so great to have a best friend is sometimes, like right now, Cal and I are thinking the very same thing.

Chapter Twenty

The baptism must be done tonight because tomorrow the lady from social services will come for Zachary. It's our going-away gift to him. Cal says he'll take care of recruiting Kate. I'm assigned Malcolm and Ferris.

First I've got to mow the Pruitts' yard. Instead of starting at eight, I set my alarm for five-thirty so I'm at their house by six. After letting myself in through the back gate, I begin picking up apples. There are less than usual, and I'm able to start mowing by six-thirty.

One minute into mowing, Miss Myrtie Mae stands on the porch, her hands planted on her hips. She wears a green terry-cloth robe and a hot pink scarf tied around her head with a few pinwheels of hair bound by bobby pins sticking out. Her arms wave high, crossing each other at the wrists. I cut the engine and walk over to her.

"Tobias Wilson! What on earth are you doing out here at this hour?"

As I get closer, I notice her face and her collarbone shine like she has bathed in corn oil. She sees me studying her and pulls the scarf over the exposed pin curls.

"You caught me in my beauty routine. I always grease up with Oil of Olay on Thursday evenings." She wipes her cheek with the back of her hand. "Are you trying to wake up the entire town?"

"No, ma'am. I've a long day ahead of me and I figured since Mr. Henderson next door is practically deaf, it wouldn't bother him much. And you live on the corner, so there isn't anybody on the other side."

Her face pinches up. "You reckon you could start with the weeding first? Then Brother can get a few more winks."

I'd forgotten about the Judge. "Yes, ma'am. Sorry, Miss Myrtie Mae. I wasn't thinking."

"Well, see to it that you do next time."

"Yes, ma'am." I look down and notice her bare feet. It's weird to see her without those pointy shoes. And the funny thing is her toes form a *V* as pointed as her pumps. She turns back toward the house, adjusting her scarf on the way.

By ten, I'm finished. After Miss Myrtie Mae points

out the patch of mint I accidentally mowed over, she tells me to come in the house so she can pay me. While I wait for her, I study the pictures on the round table. When she returns, I ask her about the pretty girl.

"That's a girl I used to know a long time ago. Now she has to grease up with Oil of Olay once a week to look halfway decent."

I'm almost afraid to ask about the two boys in the picture, but I do anyway. "One of them is Brother. But don't you recognize the other?"

"No, ma'am."

"It's your grandfather, Toby. Theodore Joseph Hopkins. Or as we knew him—T.J."

"I didn't know the Judge and Grandpa were good friends."

"Heavens, no! They couldn't stand each other! It was just the best picture we had of Brother as a boy." She squints, studying me. "You know, Toby, you kind of favor your grandfather."

As I step onto the porch, a baseball rolls to my feet. I look over, and it's the Judge who has bowled it my way. He's a mere skeleton wearing tan pajamas and leather slippers. I glance at my watch, knowing the tasks I have ahead of me. But something won't let me take that next step off the porch.

I grab the ball. "Want to catch a few, Judge?"

A few seconds later we're tossing the ball back and forth. He throws pretty good, but his reflexes are slow and he misses every one of my pitches. He takes forever walking toward the ball, and I'm hoping his back doesn't give out as he squats to pick it up each time.

As we toss back and forth, something comes to me. Dad and I used to toss the ball in the backyard. I was only five or six, but he bought a mitt, small enough to fit my hands. At first he stood only a few feet from me, and I told him that he was too close. Of course, as soon as he stepped back, I couldn't catch the ball. Gradually he sneaked a few steps toward me. He thought I didn't see, but I did.

The Judge waits for another toss, but this time I step closer. And for once he catches the ball. Then he smiles real big, slips the ball in his pocket, and whistles on the way back to the porch.

Ferris is writing today's lunch special on the chalkboard: Liver and Onions, Mashed Potatoes and Green Beans.

"Hey, Toby. Won't need you for the dishes today. Ima Jean got over the flu."

"I know. I came to ask you a favor."

He puts down the chalk and brushes the white dust from his fingers onto his pants. "I'm listening."

"I need you to baptize someone."

Ferris grips the counter. "Whoa, son! The preacher is down the road at the parsonage."

"It can't be Reverend Newton."

"I'm not a preacher, Toby."

"But you almost were."

"Almost and is ain't the same."

"Don't you know how to do it?"

He shakes his head and pulls out the tray of salt and pepper shakers from under the counter. "What is all this about?"

"Zachary. He promised his mom he'd get baptized. Then she died."

"Why can't you ask Reverend Newton to do it?"

"Because he'd want to use the baptistery."

Ferris chuckles. "He's mighty proud of that tank."

"If word gets out, Ferris, there will be a crowd like—"

"Like when his momma died?"

"Right."

He scratches his chin. "Well, how in the world would you baptize that boy without a baptistery?"

"Gossimer Lake."

"Nope." Ferris starts putting the salt and pepper shakers on the tables.

"It's the only way."

"No one is supposed to be down there doing anything. Sorry excuse for a lake, but I don't make the laws."

"We're going to do it at sundown."

Ferris shakes his head again. "Nope. No, sir. Count me out."

"Ferris, we need you. Please be there. Sundown at Gossimer Lake." I leave, hoping my words will bother his conscience. Because it won't work without Ferris. It won't work at all.

Malcolm is easier to persuade. He's just finished mowing the school grounds when I get there. He pulls a handkerchief from his pocket and wipes the layer of sweat glistening on his red face.

After explaining our plan, I tell him, "You're the strongest person we know." I almost gag, but it's the truth.

"Well, I do work out." Malcolm locks his hands behind his thick neck, making sure I get a good view of his biceps.

"You can't tell anyone, Malcolm. Not even your mom."

"Why would I tell her?"

I stare at him and he blushes. "I won't tell her."

Before walking away, I say, "Sundown."

"Sundown," he repeats.

At home, I get my Bible and pull out the paper with the verse Miss Myrtie Mae gave me. If Ferris doesn't show up, it might have to do. I look up *baptism* in the concordance and find Scriptures about Jesus' baptism. I read the verses, scouting for something to say if we have to do it alone. But as I read the story, I forget about searching for verses. I read that Jesus goes to John the Baptist and asks to be baptized, but John doesn't think he's worthy enough to baptize Jesus. Then Jesus says, "Suffer it to be so now: for thus it becometh us to fulfil all righteousness." So John baptizes him.

I grab the phone and dial the number I've known since Mom started working there five years ago.

Ferris answers. "Bowl-a-Rama."

"Ferris," I say, "Matthew 3:14–15."

"Toby, I told you no."

"Read it, Ferris." And I hang up before he has a chance to say no again.

Chapter Twenty-one

I'm feeling jumpy. It's four o'clock, and I should be memorizing Bible verses for tonight in case Ferris doesn't show, but my mind won't settle on the words.

Outside my window, Cal and Kate pull into the driveway from finishing their work in the fields. Mr. Garcia's truck is parked outside their yard, and Juan is in the back waiting with the other workers, a bandanna tied around his neck. Each wears a white T-shirt and long pants, but the workers are different ages—the youngest looks about ten years old. The oldest looks like a grandfather.

Mr. Garcia returns to the truck after Mr. McKnight hands him an envelope with the cash to pay the workers. Last December, Mr. McKnight took all the workers to Clifton's Dry Goods and bought them shoes. Now that I think about it, that doesn't seem too stingy.

Juan unties his bandanna and wipes the back of his neck. As the truck pulls out of the driveway, he looks up at my window and greets me with a jerk of his head. I wave back.

At sundown I gather my Bible and Miss Myrtie Mae's verse. Outside, Kate and Cal are waiting for me in the truck.

"I hope we're doing the right thing," Kate says as she puts the truck in reverse.

Together we ride to Zachary's trailer. Antler has rolled up the streets for the night. All the shops are closed, and Earline is pulling out of the real estate office in her old Volkswagen. The muffler roars and spits down the road long after she disappears. Under the elm Wylie Womack closes his giant umbrella above his stand. One by one, he places the syrup bottles in a box.

Cal and I get the steps out of the pickup truck, then the three of us knock on Zachary's door. It takes him only a minute to answer.

"What's wrong?" Zachary asks.

Kate steps forward and says, "Zachary Beaver, we're here to take you to your baptism."

Zachary backs away from the door. "What?"

"Your baptism," Kate explains. "It's what you want, Zachary. You know it is. Let us help you."

He shakes his head, his eyes wide. "I'm not going to any church." He backs up until he bumps into the love seat.

"You're not," I say. "*We're* going to do it."

"How?" he asks.

"We have it all planned," Cal says. "Trust us."

And all of a sudden I feel nervous because I can't remember one word of the Bible. And I don't remember where to find the story about John the Baptist.

Zachary looks at Kate, then at Cal and me. "Okay," he says, and the word comes out so small that I wonder if I imagined he said it. But he lifts the gold box from the shelf and steps toward us, and now I know I heard right. Across the parking lot, Wylie watches us as he finishes packing up the bottles and cups.

Zachary squeezes through the door, following us toward the truck. His breaths come short and fast like he's climbing a mountain, and he must rest after each step he takes. We get in after him. Kate waits and doesn't slip behind the steering wheel until she sees Zachary safely seated. Then she gets in and turns the key. Only nothing happens. "Rats!" she snaps, and tries again.

Cal leans around the cab, sticking his head in the window. "Are you sure you have it in park?"

"Of course. Now hush—I'm trying to concentrate."

Again and again she tries, but the engine at most makes a weak starting sound, each time dying, along with our plan.

Wylie rides up in his golf cart. "Need a ride?" he asks in a brittle, raspy whisper, and they're the first words I've heard Wylie Womack say in five years.

"Oh, could you, Wylie?" Kate asks as if Wylie speaking was nothing out of the ordinary. Ten minutes later Wylie crosses the street to the Sunset Motel, his wheelchair humming in the night air.

With his belly pressing against the golf cart's dashboard, Zachary takes up most of the room, causing Kate's skinny behind to hang halfway off the seat. Cal and I have no choice. We walk behind the cart, heading toward the lake.

When we pass the Bowl-a-Rama, I notice the cafe light on. I wonder if Ferris is in his room, reading his Bible or drinking a glass of Jim Beam.

Kate turns right toward the lake. The wheels on her side raise off the ground, and Wylie's syrup bottles rattle in the box. But the tires lower once Kate straightens the steering wheel.

At the lake there is no sign of Ferris, but Malcolm waits, pacing and swinging his arms. "What took you so long?" he asks, his voice quivering.

"We're here now," I say. "Don't get scared."

"I'm not scared," he says. "I was just wondering what was taking you so long."

"What's next?" Cal asks.

Everyone looks at me. My stomach rumbles like it does when I have to read the Bible aloud in Sunday school. And now I'm even more nervous because I don't want to mess this up. Flipping through the Bible, I search for the verses. Were they in Matthew, Mark, Luke, or John?

A thick figure limps toward us, the moon casting a glow behind him. It only takes a second to realize the figure dressed in a dark suit and clip-on tie with a Bible in his hand is Ferris. As he nears, I notice he's clean shaven and his hair is slicked back with some kind of smelly tonic. "I'm sorry I'm late."

I smile and punch his shoulder. "You're not late, Ferris. You're right on time."

Kate slips off her sandals and helps Zachary take his shoes off. Then she holds his hand and guides him into the lake until she's waist deep. The water fills Zachary's tent-shirt like a balloon. The rest of us shuck off our shoes and follow them. Cal and I move to one side of Zachary; Kate and Malcolm are on the other. Ferris leaves the Bible on the ground and wades into the water until he's directly in front of Zachary.

When we're in our positions, Ferris asks Zachary if he wants the long version or the short.

"Will it work just as well with the short?" Zachary asks.

"Yes, sir," Ferris says. "It's a personal preference."

"Short is fine," Zachary says. "I'm getting cold standing out here."

"What's your middle name?" Ferris asks.

Zachary frowns. "Why do you need to know that?"

"To make it official and all."

Zachary pauses a long time before uttering a sound. When he does, it comes out so soft, I wonder if anyone heard it.

"Alvin?" Ferris asks.

"No, Elvis," Zachary says.

"Elvis?" Cal snickers.

Kate gives Cal the eye.

"Well," says Cal, "I guess other people are named Elvis."

"That's a fine name," Ferris says, then clears his throat. He sighs and closes his eyes. I wonder if he's praying. Then he opens them. "Do you, Zachary Elvis Beaver, take the Lord Jesus Christ as your Savior?"

"Yes," Zachary whispers.

"I can't hear ya," Ferris says.

"Yes!" shouts Zachary.

"That's the way," Ferris says. "I baptize you in the name of the Father, the Son, and the Holy Ghost. Whosoever shall believeth in him shall not perish but shall have everlasting life. Amen." Ferris gets behind Zachary, and we hold on to his sides.

Zachary suddenly grabs Kate's arm.

"Don't be afraid," Kate whispers. "We won't drop you."

Zachary takes a deep breath, pinches his nose, and shuts his eyes. As we lower him into the water, I can't help thinking how with five people Zachary doesn't seem that heavy at all, but then we have to lift him up and I quickly change my mind. I grit my teeth and pull. Every vein in my face feels like it could burst, and my arms feel like they're going to snap.

Across from me, Kate bites down on her lip as she tries to lift him. Cal keeps muttering, "Come on, come on, come on."

Even Ferris has a look of panic on his face. Malcolm is the only calm one, concentrating with his eyebrows low and his chin touching his neck. I'm hoping Zachary knows how to hold his breath a long time, and for a second a newspaper headline flashes in my head: FATTEST BOY IN THE WORLD DROWNS DURING BAPTISM.

Just when it looks like we won't be able to lift him,

Malcolm lets out a groan I've heard only in wrestling matches. But it works. We gain a second wave of strength, and together we pull Zachary out of the water. Zachary's shirt clings to his body, and water drips down his face. He gasps for air, then looks confused like someone who got off an elevator at the wrong floor.

"That was a snap," Malcolm says, cracking his knuckles.

Ferris says a prayer so long that I know he has missed his true calling. He would make a great preacher. He ends with an amen, then says, "God bless you, Zachary."

Zachary smiles, and I wonder if he's feeling different. Because standing out here waist deep in Gossimer Lake, next to my best friend, I'm feeling different—light and good and maybe even holy.

After Ferris signs Zachary's Bible, Kate drives Zachary back to the trailer. The rest of us follow on foot. Except Malcolm, who rushes home to his mom before she notices he's missing. The moment is kind of bittersweet because even though Zachary got baptized, we know the social worker will be here tomorrow. Walking through town, Ferris leads us in "Amazing Grace." We all know the words, even

Zachary. I've sung the song a million times, but tonight it's different. Tonight the words give me goose bumps from my head to my toes. We are on the fourth stanza when we reach the trailer, but we don't finish the words because we see Sheriff Levi's car parked next to the McKnights' truck.

As Kate stops the golf cart, the trailer door swings open and Sheriff Levi rushes out. Duke is behind him.

"I was about to call for a search." Sheriff Levi's voice is nervous, and I don't even have to look to know his eye is twitching. "What on earth? Have you been swimming?"

"Something like that," Cal says.

"I'll be danged," says the sheriff, scratching his head. "Well, I know you wouldn't have been at Gossimer Lake because I'd have to fine you."

Ferris clears his throat. "Well, actually, Levi—"

Sheriff Levi lifts his hand. "Now, hold on, Ferris. Don't you go shooting off your mouth when I got important business to take care of. Zachary, the reason I came by is to tell you that your friend Paulie Rankin called me tonight. Said he'd be back for you in a couple of days."

"See," Zachary says, "I told you he'd be back."

"He said he'd been plumb over in Paris getting a new act. Something about a bearded woman."

"Paris, Texas?" Cal asks.

"No, Paris, France," Zachary says. Then he adds softly, "That's why I didn't go."

Sheriff Levi clears his throat. "Now, that don't excuse him for going off and leaving you like he did. And I'll certainly have to have a long talk with him about that. But I guess everyone deserves a break now and then."

Ferris steps forward. "Levi, I think I should tell you that we've been at Gossimer Lake. In the lake."

The sheriff winces. "Aww, Ferris, why'd you go and tell me that? Now I'm going to have to fine you."

"Then fine me."

"There's only one problem," Sheriff Levi says. "I ain't thought of a fine, seeing as no one ever broke that ordinance. I guess you can pick up around the lake for a week or two."

"I'll help," I tell Ferris.

"Me too," says Cal.

"Count me in," Kate says.

We look at Zachary, and he finally says, "I would if I was going to be here."

"Zachary," the sheriff says, "it appears you made some friends while you were in Antler."

Zachary looks at us. Each of us—Ferris, Kate, Cal, and me—and smiles.

"We made a good friend too." And it's me who says those words.

At home, I take the stack of unopened letters from Mom and put them in order by date. I open and read each one. She writes how she sure traveled a long way only to wait on tables again. She tells me how sorry she is about Wayne and how she knows he meant a lot to me. She hopes I'll forgive her for leaving, and she wants me to visit her in Nashville before summer ends.

I rip a piece of paper from my notebook and start the first letter I've written since the one I wrote to Wayne.

Chapter Twenty-two

The day after Zachary's baptism, I head over to Cal's house. In their driveway Billy sits in Wayne's orange Mustang with the windows rolled up except for a crack. He's behind the steering wheel, looking straight ahead, sweating buckets.

I pass the car. "Hey, Billy, aren't you burning up?"

He doesn't answer. He looks straight ahead.

When Cal comes outside, I ask him, "What's with Billy? He acts like he's in another world."

Cal glances toward his brother. "He's reading a new letter from Wayne."

"What? How?"

"They came with his stuff—a letter for each of us. I guess Wayne didn't have a chance to mail them."

"I know."

"Mom and Dad thought we should wait before they gave them to us."

"Did you read yours?"

"I was waiting to read it with you."

A few minutes later we're on the roof of the Bowl-a-Rama. Cal carefully opens the envelope like someone trying to remove the wrapping paper off a Christmas package without tearing it. As if they would use it again. Trembling, he slips a dirty fingernail at one corner and runs it along the edge of the seal. It isn't a clean tear, but the letter comes out without a scratch. Cal unfolds the paper and I can't help but shudder, thinking how Wayne held that very same letter in his hands, maybe hours before he died.

Dear Cal,

I'm glad to know you and Toby are having a good ol' time. Man, I miss those Wylie Womack days. Do me a favor, will you? When you're having fun this summer, don't be a soldier. I know we used to play war in the backyard all the time. I can remember building those tumbleweed barricades, stealing Miss Myrtie Mae's apples for bombs, and wearing plastic mixing bowls on our heads for helmets. Remember how we forgot them outside and

Mom had a fit because we played with her new Tupperware?

Cal, this war is real, and I can tell you right now there is no way you want to be here. In fact, it doesn't seem like anyone wants us here. Not even the people we're protecting. They just want to sell us cigarettes, booze, and anything else we're willing to put down our money for.

Don't I sound like I'm having a jolly ol' time? If I'm scaring the hell out of you, good. That's exactly what I want to do. I figure I owe it to you. After all, you're my little brother. Keep your nose clean, kid.

Your brother,
Wayne

The McKnights' truck is parked at L.W.'s Texaco, waiting for a new battery. So thirty minutes before dusk, we load the crates of ladybugs into the back of the McKnights' station wagon and stack the rest in the back of Dad's pickup.

Cal, Zachary, and I sit in the bed with the crates and we caravan to the McKnights' cotton farm—Dad's truck in front, followed by the station wagon and Mr. Garcia's truck with the workers. Even Miss Myrtie

Mae comes to record the event. She rides in the station wagon with Kate and Mrs. McKnight.

When we reach the fields, Miss Myrtie Mae springs out of the station wagon and hurries over to the back of Dad's pickup. I've never seen her move that fast. "You boys mind if I take a picture of you?"

This time Zachary says it's okay. So she snaps the three of us—Cal, Zachary, and me. And when her shutter clicks, I realize this may be the only proof we have that we met Zachary in the summer of '71.

Dad and Mr. McKnight open the crates and hand out the tow sacks. Even Zachary takes a sack. Twenty of us, including Juan, scatter about in the field.

The sun sits on the horizon, a blazing golden ball resting in pink clouds. I pull out my pocketknife and cut across the burlap, then hold the edges together, waiting for the cue.

In front of the station wagon, Miss Myrtie Mae sets up her tripod. She peers through the camera and focuses her lens. She stands tall with her feet apart as if they keep her balanced in the wind.

Kate sits on the hood of the station wagon next to Mrs. McKnight. They both wear shorts, and I can't help noticing how different Mrs. McKnight looks without her apron. I guess I thought she slept in it.

Tomorrow Kate and her mother will leave for a week's trip to the southeastern states to tromp through old cemeteries in search of lost roses.

"Ready?" Kate hollers.

We wave our arms high and Kate hits the on button of Dad's tape recorder. The Mozart sonata Dad picked out begins to play. When we hear the first note, we open the sacks and the ladybugs escape through the opening, taking flight. It's as if someone has dumped rubies from heaven. Soon they will land on the plants in search of bollworm eggs. But right now they are magic—red ribbons flying over our heads, weaving against the pink sky, dancing up there with Mozart.

Mrs. McKnight covers her mouth with her hand, and I wonder if she is just amazed at the beauty of it all or if she is remembering Wayne, standing here in the cotton fields last year, releasing the ladybugs.

One group of ladybugs soars high into the sky, then suddenly dips low like a flock of birds flying in perfect rhythm. Cal jumps up and down, waving his sack. "Wow! Did you see that?"

Everyone in the field has something to say about it, except Zachary. Holding his empty sack, he stands in his ocean of cotton with the sun sinking fast behind him. He's wearing the same stunned look on his face that he had when he first came out of the water during his baptism.

We empty the last of the sacks, gather the burlap, and head toward the truck. Before hopping in the back, I notice one ladybug resting on a lone sunflower growing at the edge of the cotton field. Instead of following the others, I guess it had its own plan. As soon as I get home, I'm going to mail that letter to Mom.

It's early Monday morning. Cal and I climb to the roof of the Bowl-a-Rama and lie flat on our stomachs, chins resting on our hands. Watching. Waiting.

The sun barely peeks above the horizon, and the stars have started to fade like dim car lights at dusk. We watch Paulie hitch the trailer to the back end of his Thunderbird and pull away. Away from the Dairy Maid parking lot. Away from Antler. Away from us.

Zachary Beaver's trailer rides down the road until it looks like a white smudge entering the highway. Even though Zachary said he'd write, I know he won't. We'd seen the last of him. I can't tell you why. I just know.

What would Zachary write about anyway? His life is made up of people who stare and ask nosy questions. But now if anyone asks him if he had been baptized, he can tell them he most certainly has. And it's even written in his Bible to prove it.

Cal stretches like a lazy cat, arching his back. There's something I've been meaning to ask him.

"How'd you know about the books and the toilet behind the curtain?"

"It was easy. Remember the night we picked him up for the drive-in? Zachary was busy looking at Kate. It only took a second to peek. When are you going to visit your mom?"

"Next week. Dad made the reservations yesterday."

A moment later Ferris drives up, gets out of his car, and hollers, "What are you two doing up there?"

"Watching the comings and goings of Antler," I say.

"Mostly the goings," Cal adds.

"Come on down and I'll fix you a Bowl-a-Rama breakfast special."

We jump to our feet. "Can I borrow some money?" Cal asks me.

"It's on the house!" hollers Ferris.

"Now you're talking," I say, realizing how much that sounds like Cal.

Cal punches my shoulder. "Hey, runt. You're all right."

We climb down from the roof as the streetlights

turn off and the Dairy Maid lights come on. Right away I notice something different in the cafe. Black-and-white framed photographs hang on the wall.

"Miss Myrtie Mae's work," Ferris says. "She's pretty good with that camera."

Cal and I step toward the center photo, but Ferris stops us, pointing toward the picture on the left. "Start on this end, at the beginning. It means more."

The first photograph is Zachary's trailer. It must have been taken the day he arrived because Paulie Rankin stands in front, wearing his tuxedo.

Next to it are pictures of the people waiting in line. I even see Cal and me. And Tara. And there's a picture of a Wag-a-Bag grocery sack. At first it seems out of place. But then when I look closer, I can tell it's one of *our* sacks that we left on Zachary's steps. There's the picture Miss Myrtie Mae took of the three of us in the back of the pickup—Cal and me smiling over Zachary's shoulders.

"Man, does my tooth look that bad?" Cal asks.

I don't answer him because I'm too busy studying the last picture. It's of Zachary, standing in the middle of the cotton field, his sack held high and his head turned toward heaven. Above him, the ladybugs look like a dark squiggle soaring in the sky. And now looking at that picture, I think Zachary is right. The cotton fields *do* look like an ocean.

Ferris stands back, admiring the wall. "I call it *The Ballad of Zachary Beaver*."

"He really was here, wasn't he?" I say, not to anyone in particular.

"Yep," says Cal, "he sure was."

And I wonder if Zachary will tell this adventure to anyone or if he'll ever mention the baptism at Gossimer Lake or talk about his time in Antler and the summer he met Cal and me.

Sheriff Levi parks out front and joins the old men for coffee at the counter.

"You boys ready for another hot one?" he asks us.

"Yes, sir," I say. "I think it's gonna be a Wylie Womack d—." I catch myself, but it's too late. Cal hears me. But he doesn't look sad. He's grinning, ear to ear.

"Yes, sir," Cal says, his chin quivering. "This afternoon, we'll be eating Bahama Mamas, licking the juice off our fingers."

And at two o'clock that's exactly what we do.

I would like to thank the following people:

Tina Lee, Bill Nuttal, James Butter, Norbert Schlegel, Tom Allen, and Jack Sisemore for answering never-ending questions;

The Scribblers—Chery Webster, Ivon Cecil, and Pat Willis;

Also Charlotte Goebel, Jennifer Archer, Alicia Cheney, and Henry Mitchell for their valued feedback;

The librarians of the Amarillo Public Library and Rapides Parish Library for their continued support;

And Jerry and Shannon—who deserve the most—
Thank you all from the bottom of my heart.

GOFISH

An Interview with Kimberly Willis Holt and her editor, Christy Ottaviano

When Zachary Beaver Came to Town is celebrating its fifteenth anniversary. The novel feels as relevant today as it did when first published. Why do you think this is so?

That's been a nice surprise. One of the reasons I believe the story continues to feel relevant is because everyone wants to feel accepted for who they are. The book is about a lot of things, but acceptance is a constant theme. We've all seen or met outsiders. Most of us have felt like an outsider at one time or another. Zachary Beaver represents the outsider.

I hope the story causes us to examine how we see and treat others. Since its publication, I've received letters from young people who've told me how the story made them more sensitive to someone who seemed different from themselves. Of course, when I wrote the story, I didn't think about that. But knowing how it's meant something beyond entertainment to some readers has enriched my life.

Toby and Cal are close friends, but their friendship is put to the test. What do you think is the most important ingredient in a good friendship?

Forgiveness. Even though his intentions are good, Toby makes a huge mistake by writing Wayne in the guise of Cal. Later he selfishly doesn't attend Wayne's funeral. The friendship survives because Cal forgives him.

Who is your favorite character in *When Zachary Beaver Came to Town*?

This will probably be a surprise to most people, but Kate is my favorite character. Kate has a heart of gold, and if readers think about the story, they'll see what a pivotal role she plays. From their first encounter, she is genuinely kind to Zachary. Because of her kindness, Zachary is motivated to step outside his comfort zone and leave his trailer. If Kate had not agreed to take them to the drive-in movie, I doubt the catharsis of the story (the baptism) would have ever happened.

War is complicated and painful on many levels. As much as things have changed since the Vietnam War, some things have remained the same. Can you discuss the aspect of war in *When Zachary Beaver Came to Town* and its relevance today?

When I started writing the book, I realized I needed to make my readers aware that the Vietnam War was going on. I never planned for the war to be a big part of the story, though. Initially I thought I'd have a hometown boy be away serving in the war. Folks could mention him every once in a while to keep the reader mindful of the importance of that war. My plan seemed a simple way to achieve awareness. Then I decided to make the soldier Cal's brother since he came from a large family. I always wanted an older brother. That led me to the idea of Toby wishing Wayne were his brother. From there, the Wayne part of the story grew into a subplot, which caused the effects of war on a community to be an important part of the book.

The day I wrote the rosebush scene was emotional for me because it caught me by surprise. I didn't plan for Wayne to die, but the scene practically wrote itself. I remember calling you that day and reading the whole scene over the phone because I was quite shaken by it. I even thought about removing it, but ultimately I chose to leave the scene in because death is a reality of every war.

Your books are created with unique characters who (mostly) embody goodness. Where do you find your characters?

My characters usually speak to me first. I know that seems strange, but I believe I hear their voices. The best way I can explain it is that it's heart meeting imagination. I have to care about all my characters, probably because on some level I care about everyone.

Like most writers, I observe others. I listen to what they say and watch the way they move. How a character speaks comes easily for me because I eavesdrop a lot. I'm always thinking about the reason someone says or does something. When you do that as often as I do, you come up with story ideas and characters. For example, we used to get the same waiter at an Indian restaurant. One day I saw him walking through a neighborhood. I instantly visualized him wearing a robe as he ate a bologna sandwich in front of his television. That's just one strange glimpse into my imagination, but creating characters and storylines is like that for me. I can't seem to turn off the "What if" part in my brain.

That doesn't mean my characters are real people I just plop into stories. On the contrary, I try never to do that. But aspects of real people can be seeds—a boy walking carefree across a field, an old man joking with his peers at Dairy Queen, my friend's sister who sang songs from *A Sound of Music* around the house. Those seeds grow into characters who bear little resemblance to their sources.

Rewriting is the key. In the beginning the characters might be clear in *my* mind, but each draft gives me the opportunity to make them appear more real to my readers.

You often write about small Southern towns in your books. How did your experiences growing up shape your vision of the world?

My dad served twenty-one years in the United States Navy. That made me a child of the world. But both my parents grew up in the tiny town of Forest Hill, Louisiana. It's a town where people care about one another and know all your kinfolk. My parents told me stories about their lives growing up in that community. They wanted us to know our roots. We also returned there between each of my dad's assignments.

For a while I got to experience that life because we lived there for about eight months while my dad worked at an assignment in Washington D.C. I saw firsthand how strong a small community could be. They showed up with food when someone was sick, drank coffee with neighbors early in the morning, and, yes, sometimes knew a little too much about everyone's business. I'm so happy for that warm, small-town-life experience. And I continue to experience it through my stories.

The themes in *Zachary Beaver* feel timeless. Can you discuss some of its themes in the context of today?
I think the main theme is acceptance. And that is always relevant. If we accepted everyone for who they are and respected that, there would be no bullying or wars.

Where did you get the inspiration for this book? Was it based on a personal experience?
When I was thirteen, I saw a sideshow act at the Louisiana State Fair. He was billed as "The Fattest Teenage Boy in the World." I hadn't thought about that event in years. But most fiction is inspired by some real moment, even if we don't remember the inspiration. Ultimately as a writer, the goal is to move away from the inspiration and allow the story to develop its own truth.

It has been fifteen years since *Zachary Beaver* was published and won the prestigious National Book Award. What are some of your favorite moments associated with the book?
I can't believe it's been fifteen years! My favorite moments occur every time someone tells me how much they've enjoyed the story. It's all any writer could hope for.

From the National Book Award–winning author Kimberly Willis Holt comes a story about family love, small-town gossip, overcoming tragedy, and one young girl who learns to find her voice through letter writing.

Keep reading for a special sneak peek of

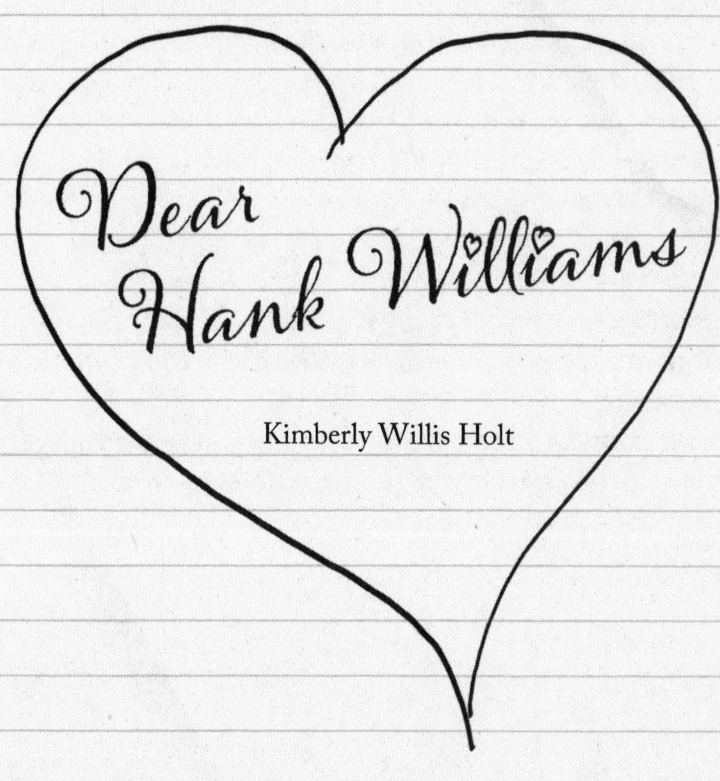

SEPTEMBER 1, 1948

Dear Hank Williams,

Welcome to the great state of Louisiana! My name is Tate P. Ellerbee, and I'm writing you from Rippling Creek, Louisiana. That's a long way from Shreveport, but our radio is tuned to KWKH every Saturday night. I've been listening to you on the *Louisiana Hayride* ever since you first sang on the show last month. When you sang "Move It on Over," swear to sweet Sally, I felt a wiggle travel down my whole body. The upbeat chorus made my little brother, Frog, and me dance around the room. Uncle Jolly said he'd heard better singers, but don't pay him no mind. He's a lovesick man.

Aunt Patty Cake liked your song too. She stared up from her copy of *True Confessions* and asked, "What do you reckon he looks like?"

Today was the first day of school. My teacher, Mrs. Kipler, is new to our school. Her glasses are as thick as Coca-Cola bottles. I guess she's real smart and wore out her eyes from all that reading. I had to bite my tongue to resist the urge to suggest Delightfully Devine's black eyeliner. It would be just the thing to bring out her brown eyes.

Now here's the exciting part of this letter. Mrs. Kipler told the class, "This year, new worlds will unfold in front of you, and you'll see your own world through fresh eyes." Right that minute I was ready to pack a suitcase for the trip. Then she said it would happen through writing letters to a pen pal.

Some of my classmates groaned. Wallace Scott groaned the loudest, but he's a bully and I guess he wanted to start the year off reminding us of that fact.

Mrs. Kipler told us we could pick our own pal, but that she hoped we'd let her assign each of us one. She promised they would be from a special place.

That minute I knew exactly who my pen pal was going to be. Guess who, Hank Williams. I've picked you! Since you sing on the *Louisiana Hayride* and I'm going to sing at the Rippling Creek May Festival Talent Contest, we already have something in common. You and I are going to be great buddies. It's funny how things work out, because before Mrs. Kipler told us about our pen pal project, I'd planned to write you a letter. The Monday after I heard you sing, I rode my bicycle over to the post office and asked the postmaster, Mr. Snyder, to look up the address for the Shreveport Municipal Auditorium. He finally gave it to me, but not before I answered a bunch of nosy questions about why I wanted it. (If you ask me, Mr. Snyder knows entirely too much about everyone around Rippling Creek.)

This letter will have to be top secret because Mrs. Kipler asked us not to write yet. She's assigning topics for our first few letters so that we can learn to write interesting correspondence. She clearly doesn't know a thing about me, because I *am* an interesting person. And interesting people always have something intriguing to write about.

I'll write again, real soon (probably tomorrow).

Your fan and new pen pal,

Tate P. Ellerbee

P.S. Tell your backup band, the Drifting Cowboys, hello from me.

SEPTEMBER 2, 1948

Dear Hank Williams,

Today Mrs. Kipler asked us who we planned to have as a pen pal. You'll never believe this: I was the only kid who'd picked one. A lot of people in this world don't have gumption, but I do. Here's the funny thing, though. When I told her your name, Mrs. Kipler scrunched up her face and asked, "Is he a distant cousin?" I had to explain that you sang every Saturday night on the *Louisiana Hayride*. She looked as dumb as a bell without a ring.

"Don't you have a radio?" I asked her. She didn't answer. She kept asking me questions, wanting to know how I knew you. "I'm going to get to know him," I told her, "because we're going to be pen pals."

Her voice got all soft. "Tate, let's talk about this at recess."

Then Mrs. Kipler faced the class and told them she had a

very important announcement about who their pen pals could be. Somehow she'd made connections with a teacher all the way over in Japan who had students who would love to write to American children.

Wallace Scott stood. "Japan?"

"Correct," Mrs. Kipler said. "Now sit down, Wallace."

He was not happy about that choice. Wallace's daddy's uncle died in Pearl Harbor, so I guess you can't blame him for thinking that way.

Mrs. Kipler's brains must have frizzled when she got her last perm. We just got out of a war with those folks. I remember when I was four years old, the soldiers from Camp Claiborne practiced marching past our house in the mornings. Aunt Patty Cake would have a pot of coffee ready for them. Before we saw them, we heard the *stomp, stomp* sounds of their boots pounding the road. When we did, we'd walk outside, Aunt Patty Cake with the coffee, Momma with the cups and cream, and me with the spoons.

The men's leader would yell, "At ease!" and the men would settle on the side of the road. Aunt Patty Cake made her way down the line pouring coffee. They'd have to take turns with the cups because we only had five, but they didn't seem to mind. Nobody had ever asked us to do it. Aunt Patty Cake said it was our small way of doing our part.

Once, one of the soldiers lifted me and settled me on his shoulders. He marched up and down the stretch of road in front of our house. *Stomp, stomp, stomp.* I remember noticing tears in his eyes when he put me down. Later I asked Aunt Patty Cake and Momma, "Why was that man crying?" Aunt Patty Cake said, "He probably has a little girl like you at home, Tate."

So you see, Mr. Williams, even if you weren't my pen pal, I couldn't write someone from Japan. I'd feel like I was betraying those men who marched by our house every morning.

Which brings me to the next point. Mrs. Kipler said in our first letter we should tell you about ourselves and where we live. She said, "You may not think you live in a fascinating place, but to other people, especially those living across the world, Rippling Creek is exotic."

Exotic? I'm an optimist. I look at a glass half-full, but Mrs. Kipler must see it all fogged up. Rippling Creek is anything but exotic. And despite that Mrs. Kipler tried to convince me at recess that writing you was a waste of time when I could be learning about another culture, I'm going to keep you as my pen pal. So don't worry, Hank Williams. You and I will be closer than double-first cousins because we'll learn about each other and how much we have in common. So without any delay, I'll tell you a little about me and the anything-but-exotic Rippling Creek.

First of all, I've got plain brown hair and brown eyes, which seems ordinary, but people say I'm starting to look like my momma. My prayers must be working. I know I'm supposed to pray for the sick and the lost souls, but I can't help it. Every night I squeeze my eyes shut and whisper to heaven, "Please let me be beautiful and sing pretty like Momma." Since I'm only eleven, there's hope for me yet. By the way, what do you look like, Hank Williams?

Rippling Creek is a speck on the Louisiana state map about eighteen miles south of Alexandria. Please don't picture a busy place like New York City or New Orleans. Most of us live in the country. Hardly anyone lives in town. The town of Rippling Creek has a post office and one gas station. You can't include Hazel's Cut and Curl, because her shop is inside her house on Fish Hatchery Road.

Rippling Creek has tall longleaf pine trees everywhere that give off a clean scent like fresh-cut grass. Even though it's named Rippling Creek, we don't have a creek here named that. There is Hurricane Creek, Catfish Creek, Marty Porter Creek, Boot Creek, and No-Name Creek. If I was mayor, I'd call No-Name Creek Rippling Creek, but I'm not mayor. When I am, that's the first thing I'll do.

For now, I live on Canton Cemetery Road in the little red brick house with the torn screen porch door (that Uncle Jolly never gets around to fixing) across from Canton's Cemetery.

Living in front of the cemetery may seem depressing to you, but the location is actually prime real estate. It's the only place you'll eventually see almost everyone from these here parts. Every few weeks someone is bound to die, and almost everybody around Rippling Creek attends their funeral. Not me. I don't go to funerals. It's not because I'm afraid I'll cry, either. I'm not the crying type. I like to think of the deceased before they became that way. I reckon they'd like me to remember them that way too.

That doesn't stop other people in this house from going, though. Aunt Patty Cake is the queen of funeral goers. Every time someone dies from around here, she'll not only go to their funeral, she'll show up at their house later with a pecan pie. And when Uncle Jolly isn't working as a supervisor at Hopkins Azalea Nursery (where they grow the prettiest azaleas in central Louisiana), he's the weekend cemetery groundskeeper. Saturdays, he mows the lawn and tidies up the gravesites. He tries to enlist me as his helper. "No sirree," I tell him. I don't want to spend my Saturdays throwing away dead flowers.

Uncle Jolly's not the only person asking me to go to the cemetery on a regular basis. All this summer Mrs. Applebud, who lives next door, wanted me to accompany her on her 2:00 visits. I feel awful bad about her husband dying, but whenever she asked, I always told her, "No, ma'am. Thank you, kindly." I can see all I want of the cemetery from my front yard. That didn't stop her from asking, though. Whenever I noticed it was almost 2:00, I hid. Thank goodness she's predictable like everything else in Rippling Creek.

Here's what I mean. Every morning, at 7:15, Mr. Gayle Rockfire drops by for a quick cup of coffee with Uncle Jolly and Aunt Patty Cake. And each school day, Frog and I catch the bus out front at 8:00. The Missouri Pacific passes through our town at 9:30, 1:00, and 5:00 and in the middle of the night at 3:30 a.m. And in case you forget, the engineer sounds that awful whistle at the crossings. Rudy Branson throws the *Alexandria Town Talk* at the end of our driveway at 4:00 every day except Sunday. And come Sunday, every person I've ever known in my entire life (except Uncle Jolly) is sitting on a pew in Rippling Creek Southern Baptist Church. So as you can see, life in Rippling Creek is predictable, predictable, predictable.

Frog is the biggest eight-year-old pest in Rapides Parish, but if it weren't for him, I'd die of boredom. And since Aunt Patty Cake won't let me have a dog, he'll have to do.

Trying not to suffer from my predictable surroundings,

Tate P. Ellerbee

SEPTEMBER 3, 1948

Dear Hank Williams,

Mrs. Kipler's big plan about getting Japanese pen pals for everyone didn't seem to go like she'd hoped. Almost every kid came to class today with a different pen pal in mind. Everyone except Coolie Roberts and Theo Grace Thibodeaux, but they always forget their homework anyway. Mrs. Kipler looked like someone who didn't get any cards in her Valentine box. I have to admit, when the kids shared their pen pals' names, I could see why she was disappointed.

Verbia Calhoon picked her grandmother who lives in an old

plantation home in Baton Rouge. Big deal! Most of the other kids selected their uncles, aunts, or cousins who live around Louisiana. The only person who chose someone out of state was Wallace Scott, who chose a cousin from Bay St. Louis, Mississippi.

You could have heard a fly land on the windowsill when Wallace puffed out his chest and said, "My daddy said you're a Red communist if you choose to write anyone from Japan." He narrowed his eyes and stared around the class like he was daring someone to object.

The room grew quiet except for the sound of a few nervous kids' desks scraping against the floor.

Mrs. Kipler stared at Wallace. She said, "The war is over."

Wallace stared back. Nobody can do the staredown like Wallace. He didn't blink once.

Finally Mrs. Kipler turned away and told us to get out our arithmetic books. None of my classmates selected anybody near as exciting as you, Hank Williams, someone who I believe will be very famous one day. I have a radar for good talent. You can bank on it.

Banking on the future of the sure-to-be-famous Hank Williams,

Tate P. Ellerbee

P.S. Please write back soon.

September 8, 1948

Dear Hank Williams,

I asked Mrs. Kipler if we had to share our letters with her and she said, "No. Though I hope you will, because I think we will all grow from learning about other people. But I realize letters are personal possessions." That's what she said, but here's what I think: Mrs. Kipler is like most people around Rippling Creek—nosy about other people's business. But she knows that reading other people's mail is against the law. Plain and simple. Mrs. Kipler doesn't want to get arrested.

Don't worry, Hank Williams, I won't share our letters. Who knows what could happen after we've been writing for a while? I might tell you some big secret, or you might tell me something that happens behind the scenes during the *Louisiana Hayride*. So feel free to write any and all gossip.

The only person who has had a response from her pen pal is Verbia Calhoon. Wouldn't you know it? As expected, she came to school and bragged, bragged, bragged. She asked Mrs. Kipler if she could read hers aloud. Mrs. Kipler looked as pleased as punch and said, "Why certainly, Verbia."

Verbia made such a production of standing, smoothing her skirt, tossing her blond curls, and reading her letter filled with boring details. How interesting could an old lady be? Her grandmother wrote about how she got her hair done and went to lunch with her old-lady friends at the capitol's cafeteria. Mrs. Kipler got a big kick out of that part. She stopped Verbia's reading and reminded us that it was our state capitol in Baton Rouge where Verbia's grandmother had eaten. When I got home, I told Frog about her letter. He fell fast asleep. The only interesting part was when her grandmother said she was going to buy her a French poodle. I hate to admit it, but that part made me jealous. It's not fair that somebody like Verbia can get a dog and I don't have a chance in the world of owning one. I'd be the perfect dog owner.

Mrs. Kipler said this week we're supposed to write to our pen pals about our family. My family would take a dozen letters to explain, but I'll do my best to squeeze it into one. I hope you don't mind a long letter.

My momma is in the picture-show business. That's why she's been away so long. She's busy starring in a film. When she comes home, she will buy me all kinds of pretty dresses and shoes. The kind that Verbia Calhoon wears. I'd tell you Momma's name, but Aunt Patty Cake doesn't like me to talk about her to anyone. I guess she thinks it's bragging. And I wouldn't want to ever be accused of boasting like those Calhoons.

I can tell you this. Momma always smells like gardenias, and she's beautiful. She has the sort of hair that women ask for at Hazel's Cut and Curl but walk out of the beauty shop looking like young chickens starting to shed their soft feathers. They look kind of blotchy. That's because they made the mistake of agreeing to a Toni perm from Hazel. Some folks say Momma's a dead ringer for Vivien Leigh. And she can sing so pretty. That's where I get my talent. She always seems to have another life going on inside her head. Sometimes I'll catch her in a daze, wearing a mysterious smile. Whenever I ask, "Momma, what are you thinking about?" she'll usually say, "Oh, I guess I was a million miles away." Now it feels that way because she's been gone so long.

My daddy is a photographer, and he travels the world, taking pictures of lions in Africa and blue-ribbon jars of bread-and-butter pickles at state fairs. You've probably seen his photographs in *Life* magazine or *National Geographic*. He forgot to pack his pair of lace-up boots, and Frog insists on wearing them everywhere, but they are too big for him. I'd reveal who my daddy is, but again, I can't because of Aunt Patty Cake. She's the boss. With both of our parents away most of the year, Frog and me live with her and Uncle Jolly.

Are you wondering why we wouldn't be staying with our grandparents instead? Well, it's the most tragic story. You see, Momma is not the only famous singer in our family. My grandparents were well known in the church world. They were Dewright and Dottie, the Gospel Sweethearts. On their way home from singing at a revival in Waxahaxie, Texas, their car got a flat. As if that wasn't bad enough, they had the sour luck of it happening right around a bend in the road. A grocery truck didn't see their car and swerved toward them. Grandpa and Grandma were killed instantly.

Once, I asked Uncle Jolly about that evening. His eyes got

all watery and he said, "I still can't step foot in a church in fear that I'll hear the choir singing 'Just a Little Talk with Jesus.'" That was my grandparents' theme song. The offering plate overflowed whenever they sang it. Sad subjects tend to stay buried in this home, so I never ask about them anymore.

After my grandparents died, Aunt Patty Cake raised Momma. She was already raising her little brother, my uncle Jolly. He's a lot younger than Aunt Patty Cake and more like a big brother to Momma than an uncle.

Momma says Aunt Patty Cake was a looker in her day, but I can't see any trace of it. She's tall like Momma and on the skinny side. Her salt-and-pepper hair is twisted on top of her head and held in place with about a hundred bobby pins. She doesn't wear much makeup herself, only a quick swipe of Rose Petal Pink lipstick (if she remembers). Which is mighty peculiar when you consider she's a sales representative for Delightfully Devine Beauty Products.

Aunt Patty Cake is like the sun. No matter what happens, you know that when you wake up the sun is going to be there. Oh, there may be clouds trying to block it from shining, but the sun will be up in the sky, a big ball of fire burning, no matter what. The sun is so stubborn, the moon has a time getting rid of it. And when the sun finally slips past the horizon, you know it's there waiting to rise again. That's Aunt Patty Cake. Some folks call her dependable and find that an admirable quality, but I think it's better to possess some mystery, like Momma and me. Aunt Patty Cake is strict about house rules. She's never written them down, but I know the list by heart. Here are the top three:

1. Do your chores without being asked.
2. Be nice to your little brother. (No matter what he does!)
3. No pets, especially dogs. (Even if it is the sweetest, best dog on the planet earth that would never, ever dig up her flower garden or poop on the porch or stink from dog sweat.)

As you might've guessed from his name, Uncle Jolly has a big belly that hides his belt buckle. He has chubby cheeks that people probably wanted to pinch when he was a baby, but now they're starting to droop south. If there is anything Uncle Jolly is talented at, it's getting his heart broken. His first girlfriend left him for another feller a long time ago. Ever since then, Uncle Jolly seems to be addicted to heartbreak. He falls in love faster than Aunt Patty Cake burns toast. (Every time she makes it!) Almost as quick as Uncle Jolly falls in love, the woman breaks his heart.

That's when Uncle Jolly drives to the Wigwam and partakes in his second love—whiskey. We know Uncle Jolly has had his heart broken when the furniture in the front room is rearranged. We'll discover sofa cushions scattered on the floor and Aunt Patty Cake's straight chair pointing legs up. He leaves a trail through the mess where he's staggered to his bedroom. Aunt Patty Cake calls it "Jolly's Path of Heartbreak Destruction."

These days, Uncle Jolly has a girlfriend—Delores Stanfield. She calls her hair "auburn," but it's as purple as an eggplant. And she may be skinny up top, but her behind is wide enough for a picture show to play on it. She's as prissy as they come. When I first met her, she held out her hand daintily as if she wanted me to kiss it. I squeezed and shook hard. Her hands were like icicles. She laughed like she'd swallowed a hairpin and said, "Cold hands. Warm heart." I can tell you for a fact, that ain't the case. So, Mr. Williams, don't pay any mind to Uncle Jolly's opinion of your singing. He can't pick a good woman or a great singer. The only thing Uncle Jolly is an expert at is plant cuttings.

Last but not least, let me introduce you to my little brother, Frog. No, that's not his real name. His birth name is James Irwin after Uncle Jolly, but before Frog learned to walk, he learned to jump. He would squat, keeping his palms pressed on the floor. Then he'd lift his behind, bounce a few times, and leap forward. He'd work so hard at it, his cheeks puffing up like a frog's. So he came by the name real honest. I have a few other names for him—Devil, Pest, Rascal, Brat, Trouble-maker, Villain, Holy Terror, Scamp, Monkey Brain. Mostly, I call him Frog.

He thinks most food smells funny. Sometimes before going to the dinner table, he sneaks into the bathroom and dabs Uncle Jolly's Vicks VapoRub under his nostrils. He claims it keeps him from smelling food he doesn't like and getting sick to his stomach.

Frog acts like he's my shadow and follows me everywhere, wearing our daddy's big ole work boots, all the time asking, "Watcha doing, Tate?" or "Watcha thinking, Tate?" I wish he had a friend his age that lived next door instead of Mrs. Applebud, who is younger than the moon but older than anyone buried in Canton's Cemetery (except for Mr. Applebud). If Frog had a pal, maybe he wouldn't be asking "Watcha, watcha" all the time.

Hank Williams, did you have a pesky little brother? If so, please tell me that they outgrow this stage.

Well, that's my family. We may not be perfect, but as Uncle Jolly says, we're like flypaper. We couldn't get unstuck from each other if we wanted. We're together through the good and hard times. Swear to sweet Sally, we are.

Until next time,

Tate P. Ellerbee

P.S. Please write back soon. Half the class has received letters back from their pen pals.